UNSEEN

SENSELESS | BOOK TWO

USA TODAY BESTSELLING AUTHOR

BRYNN FORD

Unseen (Senseless, Book 2)
Copyright © 2022 Brynn Ford
Published by Brynn Ford

ISBN: 978-1-955349-14-7

Cover Design Copyright © 2023 Dez Purington at Pretty in Ink Creations
Editing by Silvia Curry at *Silvia's Reading Corner*

<u>More from the Author</u>
www.brynnford.com
brynnfordauthor@gmail.com

CONTENT WARNING

This is a dark romance series involving triggering elements which may be upsetting for some readers. A complete list of tropes and triggers can be found on the author's website.

www.brynnford.com/triggers

SERIES NOTE

Senseless is a series of novellas set in the same world. The novellas are interconnected standalone dark romance stories, and each book follows a different couple. They can be read in any order.

For all the women who fantasize about a powerful, sexy drug lord saving your life, claiming you, and having his filthy way with you before turning you into his cartel queen…

…girl, same.

CHAPTER ONE
MERRICK

"JUST ONE LAST thing, Ryan." I reach into the pockets of my jacket and pull out black leather gloves, putting them on slowly, making a show of it. "I need you to give your boss a message from me."

"Wh-what message?" He grovels on his knees, kneeling on the gray rug laid across his sleek living room.

Ryan's gaze darts wildly around the room, wide eyes taking in the vision of horror surrounding him. I find it rather amusing, knowing he can see the wide open expanse of Lake Erie through the two glass walls at my back—a transparent view of open space that looks like freedom just out of reach.

I spare a quick glance over my shoulder to take in the stunning view of the setting sun, then turn back and note the way the lowering light shadows my men, casting an eerie orange light across the white masks we wear—a signature of the Senseless cartel. We don't wear masks for concealment; we wear them for intimidation. It's important we continue to instill a sense of fear to maintain our power, especially when it comes to rival cartels like the crew Ryan works for.

Ethan—my right-hand man—loads the gun as I hold out my hand to him, then he places it in my palm.

Ryan panics. "I'll tell him whatever you want, man!"

"You don't need to tell him anything." I tilt my head to the side as I cock the gun. "Your mutilated remains will send the message loud and clear."

I point the barrel of the gun at the center of his temple. His hands lift in surrender, only that's not an option for him. I pull the trigger, and a bullet tears through his skull. Blood and gore splatter as crimson splashes across our white masks, adding a sinister feeling to our appearance. Ryan's girlfriend, who's tied to a chair in the corner of the room, screams through the fabric gag tied in place across her mouth.

"Cut out his tongue and have it delivered to Gabriel with a note stating that he and I need to talk," I tell Ethan.

Ethan points to one of my guys standing behind Ryan's corpse. "You heard him. Get to work."

"Start clearing the house. Pick up and tag anything of value. Cash and numb come directly to me. I'll fucking know if you take any for yourself, and I'll put a bullet in your skull just like I did to Ryan. Got it?"

My other two guys nod their understanding before heading off to do as they're told. They don't need the verbal warning from me by now. They know better than to take what doesn't belong to them, and everything in this house belongs to me now.

I head for the far corner of the living room, following the sound of the woman's crying as it echoes pathetically through the space. Her hands are bound, wrapped around the back of a chair that Ethan pulled from the dining room. I crouch in front of her, looking at the face of a poor, desperate girl with streaks of black mascara running down her cheeks. She's not upset that I've killed Ryan; she's just afraid of me.

As she should be.

She's overly thin, skin pasty and pale, and she could use some grooming. But I could make a profit from her once she's cleaned up a bit.

She could make good money for me in this area—one of many I control. I reign over the Senseless from our distribution centers in the greater Pittsburgh area, through Cleveland, and all the way up our channels that cross Lake Erie to Detroit. I earned my status under the Grave Digger himself, Benji Baker.

Years ago, Benji created a synthetic drug called numb—aptly named as it makes you feel just like its namesake. I was there when he started it all. I was the first to sell for him, and I did so fucking well that I effectively hooked a quarter of the country on our powerful drug and ruined their lives with addiction.

Addiction for them means profit for us, and I rule over

my territory with an iron fucking fist. The problem is that Ryan's boss, Gabriel Stone of our rival cartel, the Chaos, has engaged me in a war over territory—and a useless one at that. The drugs we push are so different, we could sell in the same places without overlap.

Gabriel is a ruthless moron, where I'm a ruthless businessman who knows a thing or two about exploiting for profitability. We could have crafted a joint empire, and we were in negotiations to do just that when he fucked me over and killed one of my best dealers.

He sent his message loud and clear, and I'm going to send one right back—his best dealer's tongue wrapped up all nice and neat with a bow.

I place one of my hands on the sobbing girl's knee, the other tapping beneath her chin to bring her eyes up to meet mine through the mask.

"I don't need to kill you, do I?"

She shakes her head furiously. "No."

"You're gonna work for me now, aren't you, honey?"

Her forehead crinkles in confusion as her eyes narrow. "Work for—"

"Just say, 'Yes, Mr. Shaw.'" I grip her chin and move her head up and down.

Her throat bobs as she swallows. "Y-yes…Yes, Mr. Shaw."

I release her chin and tap her cheek. "Good girl. You're gonna sell pussy until I feel you've earned your place. And then, I'll let you sell numb. Do a good job for me, and you won't have to fuck for cash anymore, understood?" I push through my grip on her knee and stand, taking a step back. "Though you might decide you want to continue— the money is good and you might get used to it." I look at Ethan. "Have someone take her to Rita's when we're done here."

Rita is one of my girls—one of the few who I trust— who can make sure this girl has what she needs to work.

I make my way through the kitchen, noting the dark cabinetry and scrutinizing the design choices. I rub my bloody, gloved fingers across the black-speckled countertops.

Cheap.

If he'd been selling for me instead of Gabriel, he could've made enough money to afford proper granite.

I take off my mask as I pass through, then head into a bathroom just behind the open staircase. I flip on the light and turn on the faucet before I peel off my black leather gloves, then set them and my mask on the countertop— the same cheap countertop I saw in the kitchen. I wash my hands as I look into the dirt-spotted mirror to check my appearance.

My brown leather jacket—which happens to be the same chestnut color as my hair and beard—took the brunt of the gory impact. It's disappointing because I like this one, but hopefully a good cleaning will take care of it. If not, I'll just buy another.

I flip off the faucet and dry my hands on a bright white towel hung on a bar on the wall beside me. I'm not concerned about fingerprints and DNA because I'm untouchable—it's good to have friends in law enforcement. Besides, my clean-up crew is rather spectacular at making crime scenes look like no one was ever there, not even the victim.

I shrug off my jacket and hand it to Ethan as he appears. "Have that cleaned," I tell him, then tug at the top of my black Henley to adjust how it lays across my collarbone.

I shove the long sleeves up to my elbows, then adjust the chains around my neck. There's the heavier silver chain and the slightly longer layer of braided black leather with a circular pendant attached, engraved with my initials. I smooth my hand along the side of my head, brushing over my hair, which is pulled back in an intentionally messy knot at the back of my head.

Other than the spots of blood staining my dark jeans, I look presentable enough to walk out of here without concern. It's important to keep up one's image in my world.

"Strangulation, hanging," Ethan starts in as he appears in the doorway, "poison. So many ways to kill them without making such a damn mess every time."

"I enjoy the violence. I like to see the terror in their eyes when I hold a gun in my hand." I glance over. "Don't forget that, Ethan; it'll keep you on my good side."

He knows I wouldn't hurt him without due cause. He's proven himself loyal and trustworthy over the years.

UNSEEN

One of my men approaches to report to Ethan, his mask lifted and resting on top of his head. His expression has my curiosity piqued.

I step forward before he can tell Ethan a word. "What is it?"

"There's…something in the basement."

"What?"

There's a slight smile on his face, which draws even more curiosity. "I could tell you, but I think you really need to see it to believe it."

I exchange glances with Ethan, who shrugs. I can't imagine what would have this kid asking *me* to go into the basement to see. I've seen a lot of shit in my world, and I can't imagine anything will surprise me. Still, I'm intrigued.

I'll bite.

"Lead the way," I tell him and follow him to the basement door.

CHAPTER TWO
Willa

MY INITIAL PANIC over what I thought sounded like a gunshot is starting to calm. Still, the anxiety is ever-present—little pinpricks poking just beneath the surface of my skin keep me alert and aware, though all I want to do is rest.

Ryan must have company. There's noise coming from upstairs, footsteps creaking across the wood from where I sit on the cold, hard basement floor. The anticipation of another one of his so-called parties keeps me on edge, stirs the chaos in my mind, sweeping it into a frenzy.

I ball my fists, curling my fingers so that my uneven, untrimmed nails sink into my palms. Pain helps distract me from the fear, but the way I've been left leaves little opportunity to inflict the kind of ache I need to spare my splintered mind.

He let me sit on the floor, but he trapped my wrists in leather cuffs which hang from chains from the ceiling. My arms are stretched tightly above my head, keeping me sitting upright, nearly tugging my ass from the floor. I can stand and move my legs to relieve the tension every now and then, but I'm so damn exhausted that rising from the ground is a challenge. Instead, I let the chains hold my weight through my arms, let my head drop forward, and I try to forget where I am.

Truthfully, I don't really know where I am... or how long I've been here.

The blindfold covers my eyes, blocking out any light. I don't dare try to wiggle it off, because I can never get it back on by myself, and there was hell to pay the last time he found me not wearing it. Because of that, I'm always wearing the blindfold.

Always.

I haven't seen the light of day in...

How long have I been here?

A cold shiver trembles up my spine, reminding me not to think about my life before this.

I'm Ryan's whore and nothing else.

I'm not alarmed when I hear the stairs creak. A man was just here, and I was surprised he left without laying a finger on me. Ryan often shares me with his friends, so I've come to expect it. Perhaps the man who saw me felt a tick of humanity when he found me strung up, naked with my bare bottom pressed to the cold concrete in the dank basement. The thought of that almost makes me laugh.

No man has refused to touch me.

No man has asked my consent.

UNSEEN

No man has offered to take me away from here.

I just want someone to take me away from here.

There are three men now—I hear their footfalls on the uneven wooden steps. Their steps land on concrete, then pad across the cement floor. I flinch as I hear the click of the nearby light switching on—it's a meager light from a single lightbulb hanging from the ceiling, and I swear Ryan put it there just to maintain the ambience of horror in this dungeon.

I tense, preparing to feel foreign skin on mine, new voices whispering cruelty and degradation against my ear.

"What do we have here?" A new voice floats across the space, and I feel the rich timbre of it vibrate over my bare skin.

The quality of that voice is different.

The same sense of interest and entitlement that every man has is present, but somehow, his tone offers a hint of concern within his curiosity about me.

I must be making that up, though.

I like to think my other senses are heightened with my eyes being covered, but that doesn't mean my intuition is always right. Though it is true that I've learned how to gauge how vicious the attacks on me will be by the sounds of their voices, their intonation, the speed of their breaths puffing across my skin.

This man's voice hits me strangely, in a way I don't think I've felt before. I don't know how to take in that information, so I remain quiet and still, my head bowed.

"We just found her here," another man says, though nothing about his voice is notable.

But then I feel the man with *that* voice approach before he speaks again. There's a jolt of energy as the force field surrounding him collides with the wall I've built around myself. There's a tremor through the impact that shudders through me, causing goosebumps to rise on my arms.

I blow out a breath as my pulse quickens.

I feel him as he moves closer, so close that it makes me want to retreat. I pull my legs back, but they touch him, crashing into his warmth, brushing his leg where I can imagine him crouched beside me. Fingers tap lightly beneath my chin and my spine shudders.

"What's your name?" he asks, lifting my chin.

My lips part, aching to speak, desperate to share any part of myself with this stranger who asked.

He asked for my name.

No one has asked for my name. I'm truthfully not even sure that Ryan knows it—and I'm certain he doesn't care. But I'm not supposed to speak without Ryan present, and he hasn't made himself known yet. I always know when he's present. I can always hear him, smell him, taste his thick obsession with me.

The man with the heady voice shifts closer, the chaotic energy that surrounds him chiseling against the layers of stone wall around me. I sink inside my mind, fortifying the barrier.

"What's your name?" he repeats with a breath of agitation.

I shake my head.

"You don't have a name? Or you won't tell me?"

I swallow, and as soon as my throat bobs, I feel his large hand slip from my chin and gently wrap around the side of my neck. His thumb brushes over the hollow of my throat, and I flinch at the touch—not so much because it's unexpected, but because of the gentle way his touch lays while waves of possessive energy pulse through his palm.

"If Ryan is your owner, it might be comforting for you to know that he's dead," the man says.

If I hadn't been trained so well to be unreactive, I might have gasped.

Dead?

This man is lying.

Ryan can't be dead...that would be too easy.

I remain silent.

"Hmm," the man hums.

Something sinks heavily in my chest—a weight of desire to know what he's thinking. I shouldn't care what he's thinking because it doesn't matter. Surely, it's something awful—twisted thoughts of what he wants to do to me strung up and exposed at his disposal.

But then suddenly, he's gone. I feel the heft of his forcefield disappear, leaving my walls perfectly intact and unbroken.

"Take her down," he commands. "Everything in this house belongs to me now, and that includes her."

There's a rush of movement, the other men suddenly placing their hands on me. Only they're not groping, touching, hurting me... they're working to undo the chains. They're following the command of the man whose energy is so powerful that it makes the air rumble all around me. I can still feel him in the room, as though he's watching me.

"We need a key or something," one of them says.

"I think we can cut the cuff. Hang on," the other says. I hear a flick and a click, then that same man speaks again, and I know he's talking to me. "Hold still so I don't slice your wrist."

My arm shakes as they do something above my head, and a minute later, my wrist slips free from the cuff. My weak arm drops like a lead weight, slapping against my side. Another minute later, and my other arm slips and falls, too. Prickles and tingles ripple through both limbs as I try to move them, as the blood flow slowly returns and brings them back to life. I try to shake them, try to swing them, but my movements are slow and subtle.

Then he's back—the man with that voice—lifting my right arm in both his hands. He squeezes gently and his thumbs circle, encouraging the blood flow through his touch.

It takes my breath away.

It's almost like being taken care of.

He's warm at my side, and the heat of him is comforting. Ryan always felt so cold. I've felt cold for so long, that the warmth of this strange man draws me closer, my exhausted body swaying toward him.

"You're just a broken little thing, aren't you?" He sounds almost pleased.

One of his hands leaves my arm, and I feel his finger graze my temple, slipping down to catch the fabric blindfold still covering my eyes. A ripple of nervousness shakes through me because I don't want to see. I don't want to see him or the other men in the room. I don't want to see Ryan. I don't want to see the barren, unfinished basement where I've been held prisoner for God knows how long. I don't want to see the light.

My shoulders shrug with tension as the fabric slips. I turn, trying to lean away from his touch as he tugs it down, and it slips over my nose, down my cheeks, until it falls to rest around my throat.

I hope he doesn't try to choke me with it.

My eyes are pinched shut, nervous for the light to burn when I open them.

"Look at me," he commands, and I feel my eyes flicker with a natural urge to obey him.

I try to open them, but on reflex, I pinch them shut again.

His hand slips around to the back of my head, fingers

tangling into my hair and jerking back so my face angles upward, the light feeling even brighter against my closed lids.

'Turn off the light," he says, and the burning brightness disappears.

Sensing that the darkness surrounds us once again, I gradually blink my eyes open. There's a bit of light coming through from the open door at the top of the stairs—enough that I can see the outline of the two men standing by the staircase. I turn my head to look at the man kneeling beside me.

His frame is large compared to me, but maybe that's just because I've been made to feel so small for so long. Even though he kneels, I can tell he's tall, thick with muscle, and strong. Not just physically strong—I can practically hear the strength and power pulsing through his veins.

I wish I could see his face more clearly.

His grip on my hair loosens, then he strokes his palm down the side of my head. "Better?"

My head bobs in something resembling a nod.

He mimics the motion with a nod of his own. "Good. Now tell me your name."

I try to speak, but my throat is so dry that nothing comes out at first. I clear my throat and try again. "W-Willa. I'm Willa."

He snaps his fingers at one of the two men by the stairs. "Get her some water." One of them runs up the steps.

Water, yes.

I'm so damn thirsty.

"I assume you're not here by choice?" the man asks me.

I shake my head.

"How long have you been down here?"

I have to clear my throat again, trying to speak, and it spurs me into a coughing fit. The man presses to his feet and leaves me, walking toward the stairs and yelling up for his friend to hurry, and confusion sweeps through my mind.

What does he want with me?

Is he going to save me?

Am I finally going to be free?

A few moments later, the man's friend returns with a glass of water, handing it to him. He brings it over to me and crouches to his haunches at my side. He palms the back of my head to hold me steady as he lifts the glass to my lips.

"Drink," he commands, and I do.

The water tastes divine rolling over my tongue, wetting my dry lips and soothing my parched throat. I drink the entire glass within seconds. Then he pulls it away and sets it on the floor.

He watches me quietly, and I almost wish the light was on so I could see his eyes.

Hesitantly, I ask him, "Is it over? Can I... can I go home now?"

An audible breath escapes him as he huffs, followed by a little chuckle as his lips twist in what might be a smirk.

"No, baby girl," he says to me, "you've just come under new ownership."

CHAPTER THREE
MERRICK

I TWIST MY finger around a strand of Willa's ordinary brown hair, curious about the way my digits twitch to curl around her flesh. My hands ache to touch her, grab her, explore her.

There was just something about the way she was chained up in the basement—presented as if she were a parting gift for me to take and use—that called to the animal in me. She was used, damaged emotionally if not physically, and that's not something that would normally appeal to me on any level.

I'm a fan of shiny and new.

Yet, here's this small, broken little thing, slumped in the seat beside mine in the back of my luxury Land Rover. She's still unconscious, which I suppose is my fault, but at least she looks more peaceful now than she did in that fucking basement.

She's sunk down in her seat, her buckled seatbelt useless if we actually got into a wreck. She wears nothing more than an oversized gray T-shirt Ethan pulled from a drawer in Ryan's bedroom and my aviator sunglasses over her eyes. She fought leaving the basement, and it took me long enough to figure out it was because the light bothered her eyes.

Once I put my sunglasses on her, she was fine. That is, until I took her into the living room. I wanted to show her that Ryan was dead. There was something that compelled me to offer her the comfort of knowing that the creep who had apparently kept her tied up in his basement was no longer a threat to her.

I'm still a threat to her... but she'll figure that out on her own.

In any case, she fainted at the sight of Ryan's corpse. It should have annoyed me. It should have been enough to make me decide to send her off to Rita's along with Ryan's girl. I even thought about that consciously.

But unconsciously, my legs bent, and I kneeled beside Willa to lift her from the ground. Some part of me decided that there was something about her I wasn't aware of yet... something I still needed to discover.

Maybe there would be a special way to profit from her that I couldn't envision yet. Maybe she would be the perfect pet, obedient and blindly submissive. Maybe she would be damaged goods that needed to be fully ruined—and oh, how I could ruin her.

Whatever she could be, the idea of finding out is thrilling.

The fragile thing beside me whimpers as she stirs, her head rolling on her shoulders before she slowly lifts it. I grab hold of the strand of hair I was playing with and tug, jerking her head sideways, causing her to hiss as her hands fly to her hair.

"Don't start screaming," I warn her.

She startles more at the sound of my voice than the tug on her hair. She tries to lift her head away, but I keep my hold firm on the tangled tuft of brown hair.

She drops her hands and presses her palms harshly to the leather seat at either side of her hips, pushing down to slowly raise her body from a slumped position to sitting. I allow enough slack for her to straighten, but not enough for her to pull away from me.

"Do you know who I am?"

I hate that I can't see her eyes behind the fucking sunglasses. I'm tempted to pluck them from her pretty face, but then I'd just be met by her squinting and looking away. I prefer the sunglasses to that.

She shakes her head against my grip.

"Have you heard of the Senseless?"

She nods.

"Tell me what you know."

She clears her throat. "The Senseless make and sell numb."

"That's right." I release her and stroke my hand down her tangled hair as she pulls her head upright, leaning away from me toward the window. "And do you know who the Grave Digger is?"

Her head turns with a snap to look at me, and though it's hard to see her eyes behind the shades, I sense her looking me up and down with fear.

"Are you—"

"No," I chuckle, "I'm not the Grave Digger. But I do work for him, and everyone else works for me. I'm Merrick Shaw."

"Merrick Shaw..." My name slips from her lips as her forehead wrinkles with recognition.

Everyone in the tri-state area knows my name as well as they know Benji Baker's—the Grave Digger himself.

My eyes fall to her chest to see the heavy rise and fall of her quickening breaths. A smile twists the corner of my lips as the recognition and fear of my name strikes her.

"I take it you've heard of me?" I ask, already knowing the answer.

She nods as she leans away from me.

"Tell me what you know."

She speaks in whispers, "You're not to be crossed."

The meekness of her voice should annoy me. Part of me wants to snap at her and demand she speak the fuck up when I ask her a question. But the rest of me enjoys seeing her squirm, hearing the fear in the quietness of her whispered words.

"Do you intend to cross me, Willa?"

"*No.*" The word shoots out of her mouth with speed and intensity.

She's frightened, good. It means she'll do what she's told.

"How long has he kept you in that basement?"

She shifts in her seat. "I don't know... A long time."

"More than a few days?"

"Months. Maybe a year..."

"How did he acquire you?"

"Acquire me?" Her head turns, and she gazes out her window. "He kidnapped me from a parking lot. I was alone one night, and he took me."

"Do you think he meant to kill you?"

She hugs herself, her shoulders shrugging with tension. "I don't know."

"Fascinating. Ryan was such an unsophisticated prick. I'm shocked he was able to pull off a kidnapping like that and keep you hidden for so long. I didn't even know about you, and I know everything."

She looks over at me. "What are you planning to do with me?"

I quickly remove my seatbelt and scoot across the middle seat. She flinches and whimpers as my hand grazes her hip while reaching down to unlatch the buckle of her seatbelt. As the strap leaves her body, feeding back into the reel, she scrambles, her fear suddenly getting the best of her. She turns to face me fully, pressing her back to the door and lifting her hands as a barrier between us.

I snatch her wrists and jerk her forward, pulling her close before throwing my arms around her tiny waist and hugging her to my chest with her hands pinned between us. I lean in close, pressing the tip of my nose to hers, but she jerks her head back. With a grimace, I let one of my hands slip quickly up her back, fingers sifting into her brown hair, holding her head in place.

"I'll do whatever the fuck I want to do with you, baby girl. If I want to be kind, I'll be kind." I run my nose across her cheek. "If I want to play, I'll play." I turn my head and lick the flat of my tongue across her lips, which she's sealed shut. "If I want to use you, I'll use you." Leaning closer, I feel her shudder in my hold as I whisper against the shell of her ear, "I want you to understand something now, Willa. I've taken you, and you're *mine*. You don't belong to Ryan anymore, but you're certainly not fucking free. I own you, and I'll do whatever I want with you."

"Wh-what do you want to do with me?" she asks quietly.

The way she asks makes my balls tighten. She asks like she wants to know, not out of fear, but for clarity. She asks like an obedient pet who wants to know how to please her master.

She already knows she's mine.

My mind swirls with possibilities of all the things I could make her do for me. She's already so broken that I could easily slip her into depravity. My cock twitches with anticipation of taking this damaged girl and shattering her entirely.

My savage soul aches to find solace in the ruin of another being—a damaged spirit like hers that I can break over and over again.

I kiss her cheek, a gentle press of my lips to contrast the savagery running through my mind. "I have so many plans for you, baby girl."

I let my hand rub across the small of her back as I hold her close, my palm molding to the back of her head. I feel her fists open where are arms are pinned between us, and her hands splay across my chest. I don't know if she's preparing to push me away, but her touch does something to me. It pushes warmth through me that sinks in my gut, making me feel uncharacteristically needy.

I need to use her.

I need to hurt her.

I need to fuck her.

I need her writhing, aching, crying from the intensity of pleasure and pain, and begging me with her soft, sweet little voice to make her come.

"Tell me you'll be good for me," I command.

Then suddenly, she's trembling in my hold. I can smell the fear as it rips through her, as the awareness finally strikes her that I haven't rescued her. I can sense how acknowledgement tears through her shaking limbs.

There's a pulse of some feeling within me, something that I might mistake as guilt if I didn't know myself better.

I don't feel things like guilt or shame. I've earned my place and my power, and I have the right to do as I please. And I'll fucking do as I please, whether she's trembling with fear or not.

Though she trembles, she replies so sweetly, so submissively, without hesitation, because she recognizes that I own her now, and she may as well succumb to the fact.

She tries to turn her cheek but my grip tightens, so she stops. She lets out a sighing breath of resignation, then whispers, "I'll be good for you."

And I have no doubt that she will.

CHAPTER FOUR
Willa

THE STRANGEST MIXTURE of toxic chemistry flows through me as Merrick Shaw brings me into his sleek home. I'm overwhelmed by light and space, but more pressing is the promise of misuse and abuse. Everyone knows about Merrick Shaw—the ruthless kingpin of the Senseless drug ring.

And Merrick Shaw owns me now.

I felt fear in his arms when he held me in the car, whispering promises of depravity. But I also felt something else—something I can't identify or explain. It wasn't comfort or ease, but perhaps something closer to acceptance.

I think Ryan has broken me so effectively that it was simple to accept a transfer of ownership. I don't know what freedom is anymore, and given how anxious I feel in this vast open home, I wonder if perhaps I can ever live freely again.

Somehow, I want to go back to the dark, to the cold, to the space where I was physically chained but my mind was free. I knew mostly what to expect from Ryan and his friends who used me. Now, I'm with the man who murdered Ryan—a stronger predator, higher on the food chain—and the unknown is more frightening than being bound.

Though Merrick doesn't give me much time to take in my surroundings, I quickly scan the space to take in as much as I can. His modern mansion is all shades of dark neutrals—gray and black and navy. There's a staircase in front of us. It's steps are boxed in by glass walls on either side to serve as the railing, allowing one to see right through from one side of the stairs to the other.

I spy a kitchen with black cabinetry behind the steps, and on the right is a dark dining room, a gray and navy rug covering the nearly black hardwood floors. A couple of steps lead down from the end of the dining room into a massive, sunken living room with a glass back wall. I can see an in-ground pool outside through that wall. The gently rippling water within is clean, a perfect shade of sky blue, and a perfectly manicured landscape surrounds it.

The home is beautiful, but it scares me.

The size and beauty of it tells me that Merrick must be filthy rich—even more wealthy than Ryan—and I know that money means power. The more power he possesses, the less I have.

I don't need much.

I just want to know I'll be okay.

I just want to know I'll survive this man.

UNSEEN

With his hand on the small of my back, Merrick guides me to the staircase, and I climb slowly, weakly. Adrenaline is waning and exhaustion is drifting in. I have to stop halfway up the steps, my palm touching the glass wall at my side, and I lean into it. I partially fear the glass isn't strong enough to hold me, that it will shatter at my touch and I'll topple sideways off the steps. The sudden image of it makes me gasp, and my other hand snaps out, inadvertently reaching for him at my side.

His hand clamps around my forearm and he pulls me against his hip, steadying me. "Did he feed you?"

"Sometimes."

"Did he let you lay down to sleep?"

"Sometimes."

With a frustrated sigh, he takes a single step down, then turns me to face him. "That changes today."

Bending forward, he sweeps me off my feet with ease, hoisting me up from the step and tossing me over his shoulder. My sunglasses—*Merrick's* sunglasses—threaten to fall, so I slam my hand against them, slipping them back into place.

Hope flutters in my heart. Stupid, ill-informed hope. The thought of adequate food and sleep makes my weary mind delirious with joy. But I know why he wants me well-fed and well-rested...

He wants to use me, and that means he needs me well enough for whatever he has planned.

My frail form bounces as he hauls me up the steps. I see carpeted floor beneath our feet as he steps onto the landing and trudges down a hallway. I let myself flop against his back, too tired to hold myself up, too broken to fight.

At the end of what feels like a long hallway, I hear him open a door before hauling me inside. He turns to shut the door before lowering me to my bare feet. They touch warm, clean carpet, and sink into the softness. It feels like such a luxurious reward for my feet that have stood on cold, solid cement for such a very long time.

Exhausted and unable to control my body, I sink to my knees. I let my hands fall forward, pressing my palms into the carpet, plush strings calling for me to lay down in comfort.

"Willa."

I snap back to reality at his commanding tone. I sit back on my heels, press my palms to my thighs, and bow my head, awaiting further instruction.

"If you're good for me, I'll let you have this room."

I lift my head, confused at his words. The room is massive. There's a fireplace in the far corner beside the window, which lets in too much light. There's a small sofa and two armchairs angled toward the fireplace. Beyond the sitting area is a beautiful bed, made to perfection with navy bedding that complements the pale gray walls and abstract artwork of black and silver strokes. There's a door near the bed, which looks like it leads to a bathroom.

UNSEEN

I don't understand why he would offer this.

Perhaps it's a joke.

He moves away from me, crossing the room to the window. I watch as he strides, scanning his form from top to bottom. He moves with command, with power, with intent. He grabs hold of the black curtains and tugs them shut, blocking out the natural light. I feel instant comfort as the darkness calls to me.

He comes back, giving the rolled-up sleeves of his Henley an extra shove up his arms, and a silent gasp escapes me as I take in the lines of his hard body, as I let myself look at him, really see this man for the first time since he found me in the basement.

I might be attracted to him, and the idea of it feels strange. Attraction is such a fleeting, shallow thing that it has no place in a situation like this. I know I need to shove it down deep and ignore it, though his chestnut brown beard and the long hair tied back in a knot just does something to me that makes it hard to ignore.

Striding past me, I turn my head to watch him as he reaches for the light switch beside the door and slowly, the overhead recessed lights in the room dim. As the light leaves and the dark crawls around me, I breathe out with unexpected relief. I don't know how the darkness and I became such dear friends, but it's the only comfort I've had for a long time.

He reaches down and plucks the sunglasses from my

face, and though the lights are dim, I squint as the protective shades leave my eyes. I bow my head again, looking toward the floor.

"I want to see your eyes," he says. "Look at me."

Slowly, I raise my head, quickly passing my glance over his hands as they reach down to work his belt buckle. I lift to see his face and my pulse flurries as our gazes lock.

His eyes are otherworldly. I think they must actually be a light shade of brown, but flecks of gray swirl that look nearly metallic with the way they shine. They're a beacon of light.

He's handsome.

Overwhelmingly handsome.

I feel that sweep of attraction low in my belly.

His eyes narrow, hooded by the line of his eyebrows as he stares back at me. He reaches out and taps his knuckles beneath my chin, tilting my head, bending over me to stare intensely.

"Green," he remarks. "You have one of the rarest eye colors. It's a pity he kept them hidden behind that blindfold. How often did he make you wear that?"

"All the time."

"Well, you won't be wearing a blindfold with me, baby girl. I want your eyes." He pulls his hand away and takes a small step back. "Get up."

I stand slowly, wobbling on tired legs, and reactively shoot out my hand, reaching to grab hold of something to balance me. My hand lands on his stomach, and my eyes widen, staring at my stupid hand, wondering if I've just made a mistake in touching him.

Pull your hand away!

Yet my hand remains, pressed there to the hard muscle of his abdomen.

"Willa," my head snaps up to meet his eyes, "take off your shirt."

He doesn't look like he's angry at me for touching him. And I know better than to hesitate on a command—especially with someone with a reputation like Merrick Shaw.

God, how did I end up here?

I finally pull my hand from his stomach and reach down to grip the bottom hem of the gray T-shirt he put me in, peeling it up over my head and tossing it aside. I hug myself—some long dormant instinct to cover my naked body jumping into my mind. I was naked as long as Ryan owned me, but I haven't felt bare before this moment.

I didn't know what it was like to feel truly vulnerable and raw before now, as if standing in my naked truth before this man is far more meaningful—as if it's somehow important for my future. Tiny butterfly wings flap nervously in my belly, fluttering with a strange kind of hope.

And then he snaps, and that hope flutters away.

His hand clamps around my throat and he swings me around, shoving me with ease until my back hits the wall so hard that it knocks the air from my lungs with an *oomph*. My lips part to gasp in a breath as he slams his body to mine, aligning to my curves and leaving no inch of me untouched.

His lips skim my cheek, brushing over my skin as they travel to my ear. "It's been an interesting day for you, Willa, and I know you're tired." His body shifts and his open belt buckle rubs across my lower stomach, the metal hook scraping my skin. "But I want to make this very clear to you, baby girl. You're mine now. And when I want something from you, I'm going to have it. Whether you give it or I take it is up to you. Good girls get rewarded with pleasure. But bad girls..." He chuckles, and the sound of it is achingly heady. "Well, test me and find out what they get."

He presses his hips forward and I feel the hardness of his erection tucked behind his jeans. His hand around my throat slips upward and his large palm cups my chin, gripping tightly. He turns my head to the side sharply before I feel his tongue lick warm and wet over my skin, running across my cheek and all the way back to my ear.

My eyes droop shut, some strange, almost sleepy feeling washing over me.

Not sleepy. Relaxed.

Relaxed?

It's the way he breathes as he draws his tongue across my skin, steady but hectic—an attempt to control the uncontrollable, because I can feel the way he wants me. It's evident in the grind of his body against mine, in the way he grips me, in the sinful whispers of desire as his breath skates over my skin.

I squeeze my thighs together as I feel an odd pinch and tingle between my legs... something I haven't felt since before I was taken.

It's my own desire creeping and crawling inside me, moving across broken pieces of my soul that I didn't know were still attached. I let out a long breath, trying to steady myself, but as the exhale causes me to sink in his hold, he groans with what he thinks is submission. He turns my head and captures my lips, sweeping me into a bold, frightening kiss which demands a return.

Awakening.

That's what his kiss feels like. It feels like an awakening as desperation pulses through the buzzing vibration of the groan that purrs from his lips to mine. My head drops back with a dull *thump* against the wall as his hand presses harder, squeezing around the sides of my throat, his tongue forcing its way past my teeth.

Open for him.

Let him take you.

With resignation, I let my lips part and he devours me. His tongue circles mine, coaxing me to taste him. I let my tongue rise to meet his, and I sink in his hold as I discover his flavor.

Merrick Shaw.

Man, monster, ruthless criminal.

He tastes like the devil—all sinful sweetness meant to lure and deceive.

I was dragged to the depths of hell long before the devil came for me, and I'll gladly welcome the sweet taste of deceit if it allows me to feel this fire and brimstone melting through my core.

He breaks our kiss when he takes my bottom lip between his teeth, tugging on it before letting it snap back into place.

I blink up at him as he pulls his head back to look down at me, and it's only then that I realize how I'm panting.

I didn't want him to stop.

I'd forgotten my fate while he was kissing me, and it was... peaceful.

Staring down at me with heat, he runs his tongue across his lips, his gaze bouncing between my mouth and my eyes.

Oh, God.

Looking at him is too much. It draws too many sensations and makes me feel more than I ever wanted to. I pinch my eyes shut, keeping them tightly closed—too afraid to see him, too afraid for him to see *me*.

I hear him huff out a breath of agitation. I know he wants my eyes. His hand slips from my chin, wrapping around to the back of my neck and jerking me away from the wall. For most people, it would probably be instinctive to open their eyes. But when he starts pushing me forward, mine only squeeze tighter, determined to stay closed, and I hate it. I hate it because I know it's not normal; I know it's not right. Being blindfolded all the time in that basement has rewired my brain, and I worry it's made me stupid... stupid enough to trust him to guide me without bumping me into anything.

I only open my eyes again when my feet touch tile, which is jarring after standing on that plush carpet. He pushes me past the threshold into the dark bathroom. Standing on the cold, hard tile, I somehow feel comforted. It reminds me of the basement—it's what I've grown used to.

He moves me until I'm up against the far wall, pressing me forward to it before I can brace myself with my hands. Instead, they get trapped between my body and the wall. I turn my cheek to press against the cool tile as his hand around my neck holds me in place. With my head turned to the side, I can see as he pushes open a glass door leading into the walk-in shower. He reaches inside to turn on the tap, and I sigh, my head suddenly filled with the prospect of being drenched under warm water with fresh soap cleansing my skin.

Ryan brought me upstairs for quick, cold showers maybe once a week.

I feel as though this shower will tell me everything I need to know about the man who holds me to the wall. Whether it will be warm or cold, quick or at my leisure, with or without him. My mouth feels dry at the prospect of being without him.

Merrick's fingers curl around the sides of my neck. Dragging me away from the wall, he turns me and ushers me into the walk-in shower. A waterfall showerhead rains down from above, dousing me fully as I'm pushed beneath the stream.

It's warm... wonderfully warm.

He releases me and I turn around, my hands clasped against my body, in front of my breasts. He's just beyond my reach, a step outside the shower, but our eyes meet as his hands find the button of his jeans. Quickly, he undresses, and my gaze drops, falling to meet the thick length of his hard cock.

My eyes widen and I gasp, spinning to face away from him, though I'm not sure I'm turning away in fear of what he'll do to me. I don't think I feel afraid right now. Warm water is raining on my hair, trickling down my back, cleansing me in a way I didn't know I needed.

I suck in a sharp breath when I feel him behind me, coming in close, molding to my backside. His large palms grip my hips, and I forget how to breathe entirely.

He strokes up my sides, then down again, making me shudder. His hands leave me, then return again, slicked with soap that suds as he brushes it over my shoulders and down my arms. The sweet scent of vanilla and honey invades my nostrils, bathing me in comfort.

Inexplicably, my breathing slows as he rubs the sweetly scented soap over every inch of my skin, crouching behind me to drag his fingertips down the backs of my legs, down to my heels, and up again. He palms my cheeks as his hands rise to meet the curve of my ass. His thumbs slip into my crack as they glide upward and I flinch, tensing away from him as he does it.

"You're a stunning broken creature, do you know that?" he says. "I bet this ass will be spectacular once I've fattened you back up a little. I'll make sure you get fed, baby girl."

Why is he doing this?

I want to ask the question out loud, but the silence is too comfortable.

Standing again, he grabs my hips and spins me around to face him. Drops of water dot his forehead, tiny droplets beading on the coarse hairs of his short brown beard. It soaks his chest, water skimming and slipping down the lines and curves of his muscles.

He reaches up to tug the elastic free from his knotted hair, letting it fall and cascade down to his shoulders. He smooths back his tangled locks as he steps closer, his body touching mine as he moves beneath the spray.

Tilting his chin, the water rains down over his face, drenching his hair, drops chasing each other as they rush down his skin. My feet move me backward until I touch the wall behind me, my stare locked on his face. He cleanses himself beneath the slow rushing waterfall, savoring the feel of it with his eyes pressed shut, and I can't help but think that he looks gentle in this moment, unthreatening.

I feel tension loosening, ease running through my veins in gentle streams as moments pass and he does nothing more than stand and let the water run down his body. My eyes roam as my mind races with conflicting thoughts and feelings.

He's a work of art, chiseled in stone with hard muscles that could only have been crafted by a sculptor with visionary genius.

And I can't ignore the terrifying beauty of his cock, jutting out hard and proud at his center. Whatever celestial being crafted this man, they didn't skimp on length and girth.

A strange warmth spreads across my stomach at the thought of him taking me with it. I tug my bottom lip between my teeth a moment before he calls for my attention.

"Baby girl."

I meet his gaze to find him watching me with a sinister half-smile. He licks his lips and the warmth spreads lower, sending sinful longing and a rush of arousal between my legs.

I haven't been aroused in... I don't know how long.

"Take care of that for me," he commands, his eyes flicking down to his cock, then back up again to meet mine.

I gulp, tensing against the onslaught of anxiety and disgust that I expect to take hold of me like it always does. But it actually doesn't.

Heat drips down my thighs, a maddening river of need

rushing so heavily down my legs that it carries me down to my knees.

A harsh groan rumbles through his chest as he gently places his hand on the top of my head, spreading his legs to lower his height as his fingers slip into my damp and tangled hair.

"Aren't you a good girl?" he praises, looking down at me while I look up at him. His sparkling light brown eyes regard me with curiosity, his face relaxed and watching with interest.

I nod, though I didn't really mean to.

Maybe it's the praise—something I never received from Ryan.

I want more of it.

I'm broken, I know that. I know I shouldn't be so eager for praise, but I'm desperate for appreciation—*any* appreciation. And this is something I can do; I'm trained for this, prepared to please.

I place my palms on his thick thighs and slide forward on my knees. I see the tendons in his neck work as he swallows hard and something flashes behind his overcast eyes.

Leaning forward, I run my tongue across the head of his cock, and I'm rewarded with his satisfied sigh and his tightening grip around the back of my skull. I open my mouth wide, expecting him to shove deep inside like Ryan always did, but he doesn't. Though he shudders with anticipation, he holds still, waiting.

What is he waiting for?

My eyebrows knit together with confusion, and I close my eyes, wishing I had a blindfold on for comfort.

"Go on," he encourages. "Show me what you can do."

He wants me to lead?

Inhaling deeply through my nose, I lick my lips before opening again and taking him slowly, shallowly, into my mouth.

"Fuck," he hisses.

I let my hands slip around the sides of his legs, sliding up to hold on to his hips as I work to take the length of him into my mouth, and there's so much of him to take. Working him all the way in means gagging myself as the tip of his cock works its way to the back of my throat.

"Baby girl," he croons with a dark chuckle, his fingers tightening in my hair before jerking my head back. His cock leaves my mouth with a *pop*, a string of saliva from the tip stretching from the corner of my mouth before falling away. "You have a dangerous little mouth. I'm gonna come fast and hard, but you're not gonna swallow a drop of my cum until I tell you to. Understood?"

I nod, panting.

There's something like anxiety tickling beneath my skin, but it's not anxiety.

It's anticipation.

Pleasant anticipation.

Desire-fueled anticipation.

What's happening to me?

Without direction, I open my mouth wide and stick out my tongue, offering myself to him freely because I want this from him. And I have no idea why.

"Atta girl."

He grabs hold of my face, laying his palms on my cheeks to hold my head steady and thrusts his cock into my mouth. He groans as he buries himself deep, gagging me as he nudges against the back of my throat. He holds himself there as I struggle through the intrusion, closing my eyes as they begin to water, panting through my nose.

He stays there for what feels like minutes before pulling nearly all the way out, allowing me a moment to suck in a breath before thrusting again.

"That's it, baby. That's so good. You can take it."

He pumps in short thrusts, forcing strangled rhythmic moans to jerk free from somewhere within me as the tip of his cock punches the back of my throat.

He pinches my nostrils shut as he pulses past my capabilities. My eyes snap open wide as he blocks my airways entirely, tears streaming down my cheeks. I look up at him, pleading with my eyes for him to stop, assuming that he won't.

But a moment later, he does.

He pulls out and steps back, though his palms grip my face tighter as he bends over me, bringing his face to mine.

"That's perfect, baby girl. You're doing so well."

His lips press to mine and my heart drops heavily into my gut. He pulls one hand away, then taps it twice against my cheek, hard enough to make my eyes snap wide with alertness, but not hard enough to hurt.

"Tell me you can take it again."

"I-I can take it again."

He smiles at me before kissing me, tilting his head to thrust and sweep his tongue inside my mouth, eliciting a moan. His kiss feels like freedom, like escape, like hope that I could feel again... hope that I could find joy and pleasure again.

But even as the thrill of pleasing him pulses in my pussy, shame and fear pulse along with it.

He pauses to study my face when he ends the kiss, his gaze skimming across my features with scrutiny, and I wonder what he sees in me. He doesn't speak; he only straightens, strokes one hand down the side of my head, still cradling my cheek with the other. He doesn't have to say a word to me. I open my mouth and he presses inside again.

"Hold still," he says, and my nails dig into his flesh, holding his hips tighter as they work.

He thrusts inside my mouth with quick pumps, rubbing the underside of his cock over my tongue as I hollow out my cheeks to suck.

He grunts and groans, his sounds turning primal and guttural.

It makes my breaths quicken.

It draws blood to my core.

It makes me *want*.

I hold steady, letting him use me, letting him fuck my face at a brutal pace. My eyes are glued to his torso, watching the taut muscles across his abdomen tighten and release, clenching in time to the pulse of his cock as he swells.

"Fuck, baby," he nearly growls. "I'm gonna come." He pants. "I'm gonna come on your tongue. Don't you dare fucking swallow until I tell you to."

I close my eyes, trying hard to shut down the conflict of desire inside me. He's using me the same as I've always been used before.

Yet... I want it.

I want this.

I want him fucking my mouth.

I want him to come.

I want him to praise me, to enjoy me, to find a reason to keep me, because staying here, with him, has to be so much better than life in that damn basement.

I give a little nod, so small he probably doesn't even notice it, though I want to encourage him all the same.

I squeeze his hips tighter. I take him deeper. I suck harder.

I hold myself still for him to take, and in only a few moments, he's losing control, rutting his hips like a madman, fucking me carelessly, his dick throbbing as he comes. Warm liquid spills inside my mouth, shooting to the back of my throat, threatening to gag me.

But he told me not to swallow, so I choke it up from my throat and let the thickness rest on my tongue.

He pulls out, still holding my face, panting, looking down at me like a wild man with his mane and beard and predatory darkness in his eyes. I keep my mouth open as I blink up at him through my watering eyes. I hold out my tongue for him, showing him how I obeyed with his cum still resting on my tongue.

He bends, the tip of his nose touching mine, and it makes my head feel light. His eyes bore into mine and I can't help but get lost in the gray flecks among the brown as he studies me.

I feel his hand slip down my jaw, his thumb moving up over my chin and slipping onto my tongue. A whimper escapes me as the pad of his thumb presses down, catching the sticky substance, drawing it down the flat expanse of my tongue.

"So good, baby girl. You did so good." He pulls his hand away and stands, releasing me and taking a step back. "Swallow it down now."

I watch him as I close my lips and swallow, taking two large gulps to get it all down. Then, he comes to me, grabbing me beneath the arms and hoisting me to my feet. Dizziness ripples over me, reminding me how tired and hungry and overwhelmed I am. My knees feel weak and I worry I might topple sideways, but he pushes me back against the wall and pins me there.

He kisses the corner of my mouth, almost gently, almost sweetly before peppering a line of similar kisses across my cheek.

"I'm keeping you," he murmurs beside my ear, one hand slipping down my side. "Your mouth is perfect for my cock." He reaches between my legs and I gasp, jolting with alertness as his fingers brush across my slit. "And I bet your cunt is, too."

Pleasure tears through me from his touch, but my mind can't take it. He plays across my folds, teasing, and drawing out a pulsing ache that I haven't felt in ages.

It's too much.

It feels too good.

Two fingers slip inside me and every muscle in my body tightens painfully.

I can't take it.

I can't feel this way.

I was always able to suppress the urge to come with Ryan and his guests—I didn't have that urge often, and I didn't care to chase it. But Merrick's touch is stronger, more intense, drawing something out from deep within my soul—something dark and shameful that my broken mind can't bear.

I can't!

My hands come down to wrap around his wrist and

I push his hand away. Then I slap my palms to his chest and shove. He hardly budges, but he steps back of his own will all the same, scrutinizing me with darkness flooding the gray flecks in his brown eyes.

I immediately know I've made a mistake. I've pushed him away. I've defied him. I've denied him access to what he perceives to be his.

His eyes narrow beneath the harsh line of his eyebrows. "That was a mistake, Willa."

I press my palms against the tile at my back, wishing I could fade into the wall and disappear. But I can't disappear. I'm here, whether I want to be or not. And I've just defied the man who owns me.

CHAPTER FIVE
MERRICK

I WANT INSIDE her.

I want her cunt pulsing around my fingers as she comes undone.

She should be begging me for it, but she pushed me away, and I won't have that. I will take what I want from her.

I snatch her by the wrist and drag her from the shower, jerking her around and shoving her out of the bathroom. Spinning her, I shove her down on the bed, forcing her onto her back. Her small frame bounces off the plush mattress as she lands. She presses up onto her elbows, trying to scramble backward away from me.

"Oh, no, you don't." I bend over her and grip her bony hips, dragging her ass to the edge of the bed before dropping to my knees. "You did so good, baby." I press a kiss to her pussy, keeping my eyes on hers as she raises to look down at me. "When you do good for me, you get rewarded." I give another kiss before flicking my tongue along her slit and drawing a soft mewl from her. "And I expect you to take it."

I dig my fingers into her flesh. "You wouldn't dare think of disrespecting me with your refusal again, would you?"

"I can't... I don't—"

Ignoring her, I press in and run my tongue across her opening, drawing my hands down and using my thumbs to spread her wide. She gasps as I sink my tongue inside her, thrusting, licking, exploring.

"Please don't make me—"

My head snaps up, and I cut her off with a stern look, "Shut the fuck up and let me make you come."

Her thick, dark eyebrows snap down to form a V, pointing to her adorable button nose. "Why?"

She almost seems angry, and fuck, it's cute.

I don't think things are cute... but it's fucking cute.

I push my middle finger inside her opening, hooking it to press up against her inner wall, stroking lightly until I find the textured flesh of her G-spot. The way she parts her lips in a rounded O of surprise, her wide eyes mimicking the shape, it makes my cock twitch, threatening to swell again already.

I slip in another finger, then let my thumb fall over her clit. Stroking inside her and working my thumb, I test how quickly I can get her to that tipping point, partly because seeing her face when she comes feels like an itch I desperately need to scratch, and partly because she's actively fighting it, like she's afraid of it, and that makes me want it more.

A sharp cry bursts from between her lips as she stiffens, close to the edge. Then she jerks back, planting her feet up on the mattress and shoving her body backward along the bed, trying to get away from me.

I chuckle, putting my knee up on the bed and climbing with her. I pull my hand out so I can move between her legs. I climb up over her, trapping her beneath me, the silver chain and the circular pendant around my neck swinging over her chest.

"Didn't I tell you that you're mine now?" I tilt my head looking down at her, watching her wide green doe eyes as she stares up at me.

"Don't make me do that," she pleads with a quivering voice.

She snaps her eyes shut, as if saying the words out loud was overwhelming. I watch her through a few beats, admiring the soft, sweet features of her pretty face and the way her wet brown hair frames it.

She's fucking gorgeous.

Just looking at her almost makes me smile.

I don't know what to do with that.

I crush my lips to hers, eyes open, watching her face almost obsessively for the slightest twitch of her features.

Her eyes squeeze tighter for a moment, and something about her tension softens me. I breathe out slowly through a groan, and as I gently coax her lips to part, I watch as the tension loosens, as the wrinkles formed from her tightly shut eyes start to smooth out as she relaxes.

Gradually, she lets me kiss her.

She lets me taste her.

She lets me pry her open and see what's inside her.

I coax her slowly, taking my time kissing her, waiting until I feel her hands latch onto my biceps and her body wiggle beneath mine. She still fights it—I can feel the way she fights it—but I know she wants it, too.

I reach down between us, still kissing her, groaning against her lips. I circle my fingers over her clit, pressing down, stroking until she gasps and breaks our kiss.

"I need you to be a good girl and come for me, Willa."

She opens her eyes and looks at me, and the sudden connection feels like a knife wound to the chest, slicing into me, sharp and deep.

Then Willa's hips buck beneath me. She gasps. She draws her bottom lip between her teeth. Her features strain, but then she nods. "Okay."

Fuck me.

This gorgeous little thing was made to be mine.

I rub her faster, add more pressure, working her clit relentlessly until she's trembling and twitching beneath me. She lets out a moan and her neck cranes, chin pointing skyward as she builds toward a release. She lets go of my arms, her hands flopping back on the mattress at either side of her head, reaching out to fist the fabric of the comforter, then suddenly slapping against my chest.

Stroking her clit is like untying some knot inside her, loosening her up, taking her from tame to wild, and it's fucking delicious.

Her head jerks up from the bed, then slams back down. One hand leaves my chest and wraps around the dangling chains from my neck, fisting them, holding onto them like she doesn't want me to get away.

"Fuck, baby." I keep working her, driving her higher, faster. "Come for me."

She tugs on my chains as her head snaps sideways, as she brings her other hand away from my chest to slap over her mouth and stifle the sharp cry that comes with climax. Her entire body stiffens, and I keep stroking through her release, hoping to God she's over-fucking-sensitive. If she's a fucking squirter, too, I swear I'll lose control of my whole life trying to make her do it all the time.

I keep rubbing her past her climax, and she starts to thrash, trying to scramble away from me again. "It's too much!"

I keep at it.

"Please..."

She tightens her grip, jerking my head down with her grip on the chain, and at first, I think she's seeking my lips. But then she pulls me so close that my forehead touches hers and she catches me with her green eyes, more striking than ever. Striking, because they're glistening with a sheen of tears.

It's like she pulls out the knife she slammed in my chest before and makes me bleed out for her.

I'm fucking bleeding for her.

I might really let myself fucking bleed for her.

"No more… please… It's too much," she pleads.

My hand stills and I pull it away, reaching up to press my palm to her soft cheek, the scent of her freshly finger-fucked cunt drifting in the space between us, threatening to intoxicate me.

I brush my thumb over her cheek. "It's okay, baby girl. I've got you now."

"It's too much…" A single tear slips from the corner of her eye, dripping onto my hand.

I feel something, something more than physical, something I don't have a word to describe.

It's something like anger, but not toward her. Maybe it's anger *for* her. Maybe it's anger toward Ryan, for whatever the fuck it is that he did to her.

I don't understand it.

I don't know what to do about it.

I can't make sense of it. So instead of trying to figure it out, I tilt my chin and kiss her deeply, telling her with my tongue that I'm claiming her completely.

The only thing I know is that Willa is mine. I'm keeping her, and I'm going to take care of her so well that she'll never cry again.

CHAPTER SIX
Willa

MERRICK HAS GIVEN me more space than I needed over the past forty-eight hours. He said he had work to do and he'd let me get adjusted to my new home. It felt strange to be left unbothered.

Unbothered though I've been, he's made sure I've been well taken care of, having someone bring meals to my bedroom—full trays of delicious, fully prepared meals. I imagine he pays someone to cook for him because I can't imagine him in the kitchen.

There won't be room service for dinner tonight, though. There was a note from Merrick on my tray at lunch. He wants me to join him this evening in the dining room, and I'm not sure whether to be nervous, frightened, or oddly excited about it. I feel a little bit of everything about the man who rescued me from captivity, only to bring me into another form of captivity under his care.

"It's okay, baby girl. I've got you now."

That's what he said to me after he forced me to come.

I didn't want to. The feeling of it was too powerful, too overwhelming, and it brought me to tears the way he forced it to happen.

But it felt good, too—obviously, it did. It felt like a release from all the horror I'd been holding in my heart from everything that happened to me before. For a moment, it felt freeing to let go of it all, but when the pain and fear came rushing back in too quickly, I cried.

I might have been embarrassed for crying under normal circumstances, but these circumstances aren't normal.

I still have no control.

I'm still a captive.

Merrick Shaw has taken ownership of me.

The thought of that sends a flurry of feelings through my stomach, and it's not a feeling that I hate.

I put on the dress that Merrick had brought to my room for me to wear to dinner. It's short, stopping at my knees, and form-fitting, hugging my curves tightly. The thin straps keep threatening to slip down my slender shoulders, frail from the lack of nutrition in Ryan's care.

Still, the dress is snug enough that it stays in place over the curves of my breasts that now feel too big for my current frame. I used to have more weight on me. I used to have thicker thighs and a rounder stomach, but I've been practically starved for close to a year.

I wonder what Merrick will think of me when I gain the weight back from the lavish way he's been feeding me, whether he likes me better this way, unhealthily thin. I wonder if he'll like me less if my body changes, if he'll look at me one day and decide he's done with me.

What will he do with me when he's done with me?

Will he kill me?

Will he send me back to my life before?

It wasn't much of a life before.

Single.

Depressed.

One missed paycheck away from homelessness.

No family to miss me, no close friends to care.

In reality, I was unseen—a nobody who could die in her home without anyone realizing it for months. Ryan proved that was true when he kidnapped me and made me truly invisible to the world.

Maybe it would be better if Merrick kills me when he's through. It's not like I could afford the trauma therapy I would need to function independently, anyway. The thought has me laughing darkly to myself as I pull up the slipping strap of my red dress.

I didn't do anything to my hair, and though my brown strands are naturally thick and wavy, it almost looks too plain against the fancy red dress and strappy high heels. Merrick had left make-up for me, too, but I didn't really feel like putting any on. I couldn't stand the thought of putting on a cakey layer of foundation, or exhausting my unsteady hands trying to draw on my eyeliner just right.

I did put on the red lipstick, though. My lips looked pale in the mirror, and the lipstick color matched the dress so well that I decided to put some on. I am a little worried that Merrick will be upset that I didn't use every ounce of make-up he left for me, but I just couldn't bring myself to do it. It was exhausting enough to shimmy into this dress.

At seven o'clock, I make my way downstairs to silence. I try to walk down the steps on my toes so my heels don't touch and click against the hard floors—I'm not interested in making my presence known immediately through such silence.

As I descend the glass-enclosed staircase, my gaze naturally travels to the front door only steps ahead. My feet touch the landing and I pause, staring, wondering whether I should open the door and walk through it, try to make a run for it.

How far would I get?

I don't recall whether the driveway was long. I don't recall whether his home was gated or if there were security cameras or guards. I have to suspect there would be for a man of his status.

Do I even want to try?

Do I really want to escape this for the life I had before?

"You're welcome to walk out that door."

I'm startled, nearly jumping out of my skin at the sound of Merrick's commanding voice. My hand leaps to press over my heart, which has skipped a beat, and I turn toward him as he saunters through the dining room to my left. His presence sucks all the oxygen from the room and I forget to breathe.

His chestnut-brown mane is pulled back in a knot at the back of his head. The collar of his black button-up is open to show the silver chain and black leather braided necklace he wears. His sleeves are rolled up to his elbows, revealing the broad musculature of his frame through the taut lines and ridges of his forearms.

He stops right in front of me, standing and staring down at me. "You can walk out if you want to, Willa. But I will come after you and bring you back."

It's the illusion of a choice, then.

He reaches out to pluck a strand of my hair and slowly runs his finger down the length. "You look stunning in this dress."

The way his eyes scan me makes me feel something strange, something that makes me wonder whether I actually care to leave.

I can't recall a time when a man looked at me like that. There's a hunger in his light brown eyes but swirling through his curious features is an expression of interest— the look someone gives when you know they want to ask you a question, but they're nervous about your response, and so they never ask.

It's strange, but I like the way it makes me feel—as if I have some tiny parcel of power with him so long as he continues to look at me like that.

A look like that could be healing...

A look like that almost makes me want to stay.

I reply quietly, "Thank you."

He takes a step back, sweeping out his arm to show me the dining table behind him. "Come, sit, eat."

He walks around the table as I move into the dark dining room. He moves to a seat at the far end and pulls out the chair for me. I offer him a small smile before lowering to sit, that odd flurry of feelings kicking up in my stomach again at the perceived kindness he shows me. I settle into my seat as he moves, sitting opposite me at the head of the table, four seats along the sides between us.

I look down at the full plate of food already in front of me, and my stomach rolls with hunger. I look up at him hopefully, and he picks up his fork.

"You don't need to wait for my permission to eat when you're hungry, Willa. Go on."

I don't hesitate, picking up my fork and knife, slicing into the juicy steak before me. I lift the fork to my lips and take a bite, savoring the flavor with a sigh as it rolls on my tongue. Lifting my gaze from my plate, I see him watch me with that curious look.

He finishes one bite, then sets his fork down before leaning back in his chair. "What happened to you in that basement?"

I gulp down my bite, half-chewed, and though it goes

down, it drags down my throat. I cough against it, reaching for the glass of wine and quickly bringing it to my lips, drinking too much, too quickly to wash away the lump in my throat.

Merrick watches me and waits, his head cocked to the side. "You okay, baby girl?"

I cough once more, take another sip, then nod. I'm fine, but he caught me by surprise with the question I don't want to answer. Still, he watches me, waiting expectantly for me to respond.

"I really don't want to talk about what happened in the basement." I drop my eyes to my plate so I don't have to look at him.

I sense him shift in his seat, leaning forward. "That's not a choice. I'm asking you what happened, and I expect you to tell me."

I raise my chin and boldly ask, "And what happens if I don't?"

His grin broadens, and he swipes a hand over his short beard. "Fuck around and find out."

His words float right through my stomach, sinking heavily, causing an equal mix of anxiety and desire.

Desire?

I press my suddenly sweaty palms to my thighs, rubbing over the fabric of my dress. Looking down at my plate, I tell him, "I was used."

"Used how?"

I swallow. "For... sex."

The word doesn't sound right. It wasn't sex. It was too violent and disgusting to call it that, but I struggle to get out the words, to express it as assault of the vilest nature.

"Was it just Ryan who used you?"

"Ryan and his friends. He'd have friends over on the weekends. He'd bring me out for parties."

"And what...? They would just take turns with you?"

I raise my eyes to look up at him from beneath my lashes. "Yes. Please don't make me go into specifics."

"Ryan was a piece of shit," he confirms what I already knew, but something about the look in his narrowed eyes calls to me, drags my attention to him, forces me to lift my head and look at him fully. "He deserved the bullet I put in his head. He can't hurt you anymore. No one's going to hurt you again."

"You can't make a promise like that. No one can."

His jaw ticks, eyebrows slanting toward his nose and forehead wrinkling as if he's confused that I would think that. "I can. I can promise you the fucking world, and you can be damn sure I'll deliver."

Merrick is so full of himself—cocky, dangerously arrogant, though I would never say that to him. Yet the strength of his overconfidence does something to me. It coils inside me, wrings me out, dripping bliss through my center. To think of someone so strong, so powerful, promising me the whole damn world...

It almost makes me feel important.

"Why would you promise me anything? What are you planning to do with me?"

With a flurry of noise, his utensils clang, and his plate scrapes against the table as he shoves it all aside, clearing the spot in front of him. "Get on the table."

"What?"

"Get on the fucking table, Willa. If you'd like an answer to your question, then crawl to me."

I'm afraid to know the answer, but my need to know is far stronger. And there's just something about the way he stares at me that calls to me. It's like his stare reaches inside me, plucks a string inside my chest, and yanks me in his direction.

Ryan had me trained to move when he commanded, and I did it to avoid pain. But moving on Merrick's command feels decidedly different.

It *is* different...

It's different because I can feel that he's actually giving me the choice. If I wanted to stay put and allow my question to go unanswered, I think he would allow it. And the understanding of that choice makes me want to follow his command.

I stand, then climb onto the table. On my hands and knees, I crawl to him, fully aware of my vulnerability. He can see right down my dress through my cleavage, and he does nothing to hide his blatant stare. It heats me, and I can feel my cheeks pinken with a touch of embarrassment...but also, excitement.

Merrick's eyes raise to meet mine, and he holds me in his gaze, steadily drawing me closer. He calls to me without a word, and the closer I get, the heavier I feel. Heavier in my mind, my heart, my soul. Heavier through my breasts, aching to be squeezed. Heavier for the unexpected wetness pooling between my legs.

The sharp rise and fall of his chest as he waits for me shows his desire...desire for *me*. Not just because I'm a strung up piece of meat with warm holes to fuck, but because there's something he sees in me that calls to him.

Something I see in him calls to me, too, and I have to admit to myself that I crave it—I crave *him*.

It's unexplainable.

It's insane.

But it makes me feel more powerful than I've ever felt in my pathetic life, and I don't want to let go of that feeling.

I want him to want me.

I want to want him.

There's no sense in fighting this craving we have for each other.

CHAPTER SEVEN
MERRICK

WILLA IS MINE.

I claimed her the moment I laid eyes on her, but there's no doubt in my mind that she's just claimed me, too. It's the way she obeyed, the way she stood with such determination, climbed onto the table, and started crawling…just the way I asked her to.

I'm a smart man. I understand the twisted psychological elements at play here with her fragile mind. Ryan had broken her to submit, probably to spare her pain and punishment. I'm the man who rescued her, fed her, gave her a warm bed and a safe place to sleep. She wants to be grateful to the man who saved her, and her natural submissiveness leads her to follow my command without a fight.

But there's more than that behind her eyes as she crawls to me, more than a broken mind seeking comfort and praise from the man who saved her.

There's passion there, a burning green inferno in her eyes.

There's desire.

There's excitement mingling with the pulse of her anxiety, and it's the exact mixture I want from her. In my presence, I want her equally high on anticipation and fear.

She comes to a stop in front of me, sitting back on her heels. I watch the way her heavy tits rise and fall with her quickened breaths, the way her thick nipples peek through the fabric of her dress.

"Ass on the table," I tell her, "Legs over the edge."

She lets out an audible breath as her legs scramble beneath her to do what I said. As soon as she settles with her feet dangling in front of me, I push back in my chair and wrap my hand around her ankle, lifting her leg to my lips so I can kiss my way up the length of it.

"What are you doing?" she asks in her sweet little voice.

"Having dinner."

"I thought you were going to answer my ques—"

"Yes, your question. What am I planning to do with you?" I kiss the inside of her thigh, slowly moving closer to the apex of her legs. "I'm planning to spend as much time as I can between your thighs."

"For...for how long?" She chokes out the words.

I raise my head to look up at her. The anxiety in her voice tells me she's not asking how long I'm about to spend between her thighs. She's asking how long I'm going to keep her. I can see the fear in her green eyes, fear that she's disposable. She has yet to understand the depth of my obsession and the strength of my loyalty.

Gently, I lower her leg, pushing her knees apart wider. I scoot in between them, grabbing her hips and sliding her ass closer to the edge. "I don't make decisions lightly, Willa, and when I stake a claim, it's forever, set in stone, unchanging."

I push my hands up her sides, smiling at the way her body tenses and twitches with my touch. I play my fingers along the edge of her dress, across her chest, hooking the fabric, then sharply tugging down to expose her breasts. She gasps as I rub my thumb across one of her dark nipples.

"I claimed you when I killed him, and you're mine forever. Like it or not, you'll never be free of me."

I lean in and swipe my tongue flat across her nipple. Her head drops back as she whimpers, one hand dropping behind her to lean on the table, the other landing on the side of my head. I take that nipple into my mouth, sucking it in, rolling my tongue around it, nipping it with my teeth. I play until she's twitching and gasping, trembling and begging, with her ass sliding forward along the table.

I pull back to look at her, and the way she gazes down at me makes my cock hard without a single touch. Her green eyes are hooded and darkened, bright, red-painted lips parted and panting. I grip her thighs and give them a good squeeze before quickly trailing up, shoving the fabric of her skirt toward her hips.

I reach beneath to grab her panties. She leans back on her arm, and the sharp heels of her shoes dig into my thighs as she lifts her ass, letting me push her skirt all the way up to her waist, and slip off her panties.

I bring them to my nose and inhale deeply, my eyes closing in bliss at the smell of her sex. I've always loved the smell of it, but Willa's scent drives me mad. It's the perfect swirl of sweetness and filth—just like her—that has a tremor rippling down my spine.

I stand briefly to shove her underwear into my pocket, knowing that I won't be giving these back to her.

I lick my lips as I sit back down and take in the sight of her glistening pussy before me, a perfectly delicious feast laid out before me on my dinner table.

Suddenly, I'm starving.

I dip my head between her legs and lick her cunt with a long drag of my tongue from the end of her slit all the way up to her clit. She whimpers as I raise one of her legs over my shoulder, moans as I press my entire face into her wet pussy and eat her hungrily, sloppily, with no intent other than to taste every bit of her until I've had my fill.

She moans and gasps, twitching and tightening, begging and pleading for me to make her come before long. It's a different song than she was singing when I fucked her with my fingers the other day, when I forced her to come and she cried. She wants it now, desperately…maybe as desperately as I want it.

I want her.

All of her.

I won't stop until she's ruined completely, until she's so broken that she could never find pleasure or joy with anyone other than me. I'll make sure I'm the only man she ever wants.

My fucking cell phone starts ringing, vibrating in my back pocket. "Fuck," I mutter against her pussy.

I need to take the damn call, but I'm not done feasting on her yet.

I search for her clit with my tongue, knowing I've found the sensitive spot when she jolts and trembles through a sweet whimper. "That's it right there, baby girl. I need you to come fast for me. Come before I miss my call."

"What?" She looks down at me. "I can't—"

I hum against her clit and her eyes flutter shut. "Yes, you can. I'm gonna take you there fast. Focus, baby."

I wrap my lips around the sensitive flesh and suck her rhythmically, making sure my tongue presses to her clit as I force pulsing waves of pleasure through her body. I suck and flick my tongue, forcing so much pleasure through her that her legs shake and jerk, overwhelmed by sensation. I reach up to palm her tit, draw my fingers back to pinch her nipple, rolling the hardened peak with gentle pressure to spur release.

"Merrick," she whispers, and fuck, I want to come inside her. I want to fuck her on the table and make her come on my cock.

But the phone is still ringing, less than twenty seconds

before it becomes a missed call, and I need to get her there. I need to fucking finish her off.

I pull harder at her nipple, suck faster, and like the perfect little good girl that she is, she comes fast for me, crying out her release. Her knees squeeze my head and her ass slips forward. I feel the pulse of her orgasm throbbing against my lips and tongue. The moment her body goes limp and lax, I shove to my feet, grab my phone from my back pocket, and answer the call just in the nick of time.

"Merrick," I say.

I move in closer, standing between her spread legs to make sure she doesn't fall off the table, encouraging her to lay back with my hand on her shoulder. I reach with my free hand to work at my belt buckle as I wait for someone to answer on the other end of the line.

"Got your message." Gabriel's voice comes through the line, and it halts me. "You're really classless, you know that? Sending me his tongue in a box."

I smile, pleased he got the package I had Ethan deliver. I look down at Willa on her back on the table, legs still spread on either side of me, her hands tangled in her hair as she pants to catch her breath. I remove my free hand from my belt buckle and lay my palm on her stomach, slowly running it over her body, stroking her, almost like I'm petting her, and it comes so naturally.

"Really? I thought it was a rather fitting way to let you know that we need to talk."

"My fifteen-year-old daughter opened it, you asshole!"

"Then I'd say she's learned a very important lesson about touching things that don't belong to her. Crucial in our line of work, wouldn't you say?"

Willa's fingers are soft around my wrist, holding on as my hand strokes between her exposed breasts, then back down her stomach. Her body is warm beneath my palm, and the way she watches my hand makes my cock thicken with need.

I let my hand slip down her side, and my fingers curl into the fabric of her dress at her hip. I give a sharp tug to drag her down further so her ass teeters on the edge and I press in closer, rubbing against her soaking wet pussy.

"I'm sick of dealing with you," Gabriel says. "I should walk away from the fucking deal entirely."

"So walk away, Gabriel. Walk away and we'll keep fighting for turf rights. If continued bloodshed from both sides is what you want, then walking away from negotiations sounds like the right fucking move for you."

"Call your boss. I wanna talk to the Grave Digger."

"You and I both know he doesn't need to be involved in this bullshit."

I unbutton and unzip my pants when Willa tugs her bottom lip between her teeth. It's the sweet, deceptive innocence of her look that does it for me. She's a perfectly submissive little pet—it's clear she was always meant to obey.

She was always meant to be mine.

I free my hard cock and take it in my grip, rubbing the tip of it along her slit, gathering her wetness. She whimpers and I bend over her to slap my hand over her mouth and silence her. I lift my index finger from the hand that holds my cell phone to my ear, slipping it down for a moment to hold it to my lips and indicate she needs to be quiet.

When her green eyes hood and she gives me a sharp little nod, I lift my phone back up to my ear and shift the hand that covers her mouth. I shove two fingers past her lips, press them down on her hot little tongue, and drag them back. Surprisingly, she clamps her lips around my fingers and sucks them on the way out, and *shit*, I nearly come all over her dress.

Pulling my hand back, I rub her saliva over the head of my cock before slowly pressing inside her. The way I fit inside her is nothing short of perfection, and I have room for nothing less than perfection in my life.

She clamps her hand over her mouth to hide a whimper like a good girl.

She's such a good fucking girl.

She was made for me.

"You call him, or I will," Gabriel says. "I'll send him a message loud and clear that I want to talk to him...just like the message you sent me."

He means the tongue in the box—and it would come from one of my men, one of the Senseless.

UNSEEN

My job might be a crime and my entire existence runs against the law, but when it comes to the business aspect, I have integrity, and I care about the men who work for me so long as they're loyal—and I only work with loyal men. Gabriel's threat brings me an urgent sense of unease that prompts me to acquiesce.

"I'll fucking call him, Gabriel. We don't need any more goddamn bloodshed in this war you started."

He chuckles. "*I* started? Watch yourself, Merrick. It might be *your* tongue I send to Benji."

He ends the call. I stare at my phone screen for a beat, then I shove it in my back pocket before bending over Willa, planting my palms on either side of her waist on the table.

"I'm sorry about that, baby. I intended to give you my full attention tonight, but duty calls." I pull out of her, then slam back in, shaking her body backward along the table with the force of it, causing her to groan out an audible breath as her hand comes away from her face.

"What is this?" she whispers, her eyes watching me with lust and bewilderment.

"This is your future with me. Feasting, fucking, and anything else your pretty little heart desires." I reach to tuck a strand of hair behind her ear. "But you'll have to give me just a minute. I need to make a phone call before I finish you off."

I pull out and it's like leaving paradise. I think she feels it too, because I hear a puff of breath escape her, as if I dragged the air from her lungs when we separated.

Somehow, it felt like that for me, too.

I have to keep her safe.

She's like a princess I stole from a disgusting duke intent on corrupting her, a mediocre sub-royal who could never have been worthy of her. She's still so small and meek, soft-spoken and compliant. But she has all the makings of a queen, of a woman who could become silently powerful standing by my side.

The image of it makes it that much harder to step back and walk away from her, leaving her spread out on my dining room table like the best fucking feast I've ever had.

I just have to make this phone call... but then I'll be back to finish my meal.

CHAPTER EIGHT
Willa

I FEEL DIFFERENT, and not in a bad way. I feel different in a way that coats my insides and melts down the walls, hot and sticky and slow. I feel overwhelmed, charged up, sensual, and needy.

The slightest touch from Merrick makes my stomach clench with the ache of desire, but not the kind of desire that makes me feel ashamed of myself. No. The desire he inspires makes me feel powerful, like I'm wanted, needed... like I'm *chosen.*

His.

I think he's claimed me, and I like it.

Brazenly, my hand travels down my front, quickly seeking the slick flesh between my legs. He left the room, but I'm aching, swollen, desperate for more. Yet somehow, it feels wrong to put my fingers there without his command. I think I want his permission to touch myself. I know it's a crazy thought—probably from the traumatized part of my brain that's eager to please the man who saved me—and even if it is, I don't think I care.

I want his permission.

I want his command.

I want him to be pleased with me.

I want him to keep calling me his baby girl.

I sit up, then hop down from the table, my knees wobbling as I land on my high heels. I take a moment to steady myself before walking, following the path he took out of the dining room and around the staircase to a hallway beyond it. My heels click on hardwood floors as I stumble down the hallway, feeling half-drunk on this lust intoxication, my dress still pushed up over my hips, pulled down to expose my breasts, and my hair surely a tangled mess.

My palms are sweating, heart is pounding, clit is throbbing with the need to be touched again as I find the third door on my left wide open. I slow to a stop as I approach the doorframe and peak inside to see Merrick sitting behind a large wooden desk, bending to unlock a drawer with a key and pulling out a cell phone that he has to flip open—it seems older, or like one of those phones you can pay cash for.

He dials a number—all ten digits from memory instead of speed dial—and then his eyes lift to spot me standing there. Suddenly, I wish I would have pulled down my skirt and covered my chest, maybe ran my fingers through my hair to be more presentable.

He raises two fingers and waves them toward him in a "come hither" motion before leaning back in his chair, reaching down with one hand to adjust his thick erection.

As if a string were attached to his beckoning fingers, I'm drawn toward him.

I cross the distance, coming around the desk and stepping close as he swivels in his chair. He holds his finger to his lips to tell me he needs me quiet as he sits up, knees spread wide.

His palm lands on my hip, fingers digging into my flesh as he pulls me closer, tugging me to stand between his legs. His hand slips up my side, and he rubs his thumb across my nipple, causing my eyes to flutter shut, my head to drop back, and my knees to weaken.

He takes his hand away to wrap it around his cock, still hard and thick and calling to me.

A few days ago, I was a broken girl, chained up and blindfolded in an asshole's basement, used and abused and terrified by the thought of pleasure. Then, Merrick Shaw claimed me and made me a whole new woman—strong, confident, hungry for desire.

My mind is a mess, but I feel so good with him, like I could do anything without fear. He makes me feel like I'm safe, protected, cared for. Maybe it's naive to think such a thing about a ruthless drug lord, but he did save me and I do have gratitude for it.

I want to please him just as much as he pleases me.

I lift my leg and move to straddle his lap as I hear the muffled sound of a voice coming through the cell phone he holds to his ear.

"Gabriel wants to negotiate," Merrick says with no preamble, no "hello" or "how are you."

He fists his cock as I guide my hips forward, angling over the tip. I sink down slowly, gradually taking him in, inch by inch. I fight the moan that rumbles through my chest, aching to release, and he lets go of his cock to clamp his free hand over my mouth.

"He said he's sick of dealing with me and wants to negotiate with you; told me to call the Grave Digger, or he'd send you a message himself. We don't need any more bloodshed."

Is he talking to the Grave Digger? Benji Baker? The infamous leader of the Senseless cartel?

My heart pounds heavily behind my ribs as the knowledge of the danger these men pose creeps into my mind…

The Senseless are dangerous.

The Grave Digger is psychotic.

Merrick Shaw is ruthless.

The thought should shut me down, frighten me, make me want to hide in the dark corners of my mind to get away. Instead, my response is wrong… all wrong.

And so fucking right.

It turns me on. I'm on top of a powerful man, someone

so powerful that he negotiates dealings for the Senseless with other drug rings, so powerful that he speaks with the Grave Digger directly, so powerful he could have any woman he snapped his fingers at.

He found me at my worst, chained and broken. He could have left me for dead. He could have killed me himself. Instead, he took me, brought me to his home, fed me, clothed me, and made me his.

I'm *his*, and the power of that feeling rushes straight through me.

I rock my hips against him as he meets my eyes, slowly fucking him as he stares deeply, managing to maintain the phone conversation without missing a beat.

"We can meet him tomorrow," Merrick says. "At the warehouse."

He pauses as he listens, and my hips move a little faster as confidence I haven't felt in years coils around me and draws me against him.

"I'll send him the details. Right. Tomorrow morning at nine."

He pauses once more, mutters a quick sound of agreement, then ends the call. He tosses the phone at his desk a little too hard, and it skitters across the top before crashing to the floor on the opposite side.

"You're a perfect fucking distraction, do you know that?" He pulls his hand from my mouth and places both palms on my hips, his gaze falling to watch where our bodies meet. "That's so good, baby. Keep going. Don't stop until I tell you to."

My hips move of their own will while questions and chaos all swirl in my mind, a perfect storm of lust and wonder brewing within me.

"I want this," words fall from my lips without thought, "I want you. I should be afraid of you."

His hands move slowly up my back, heating me with his touch that's somehow soothing. I wrap my arms around him as I lean in, hugging myself to him, letting him hold me close.

"I won't hurt you," he says, and I believe him, "unless you ask me to."

The muscles in my stomach tighten and clench at the thought of him being rougher with me.

How could I ever want such a thing after all I've been through?

I moan as I feel him swell inside me, as his lips find the crook of my neck and caress me there with unfathomable tenderness. He groans against my skin and it vibrates all the way through me, spurring me to sink him deeper, rock my hips faster with the need to make him tremble with pleasure.

I want to make him feel good.

I want to please him.

His breaths quicken and his fangs come out, so to speak. His teeth scrape across my skin and it heats me brilliantly. I find a steady rhythm and turn my focus on him, overwhelmed with the need to make him come.

"Please," I whisper against his ear. "Come inside me, please."

"Fuck." His hips jerk off the seat, thrusting up into me, taking over with sudden frantic need.

It's almost like he wants to come because I asked him so sweetly, like he needs to come because I pleaded for it.

Fucking from beneath me, Merrick swells and thrusts and groans, and when he comes inside me, I have to pull back to watch. I grip his shoulders, angling myself so I can watch his face during his release. One second, his expression is tight with primal tension, and the next, his lips are tugging into a slow, sated smile, a peaceful relief.

We watch each other through heated breaths that mingle between us. He lifts a hand to brush the tangled hair from my face. His touch against my cheek is delicate, sweet, coaxing me to turn my head against his palm.

He sweeps his thumb along my bottom lip. "You're a beautiful creature, Willa."

"Are you going to keep me?"

"Are you going to keep being such a good girl for me? Are you going to prove that I can trust you with my life?" His hooded gaze is scrutinizing.

I nod. "Yes." My hands fall to grip the collar of his shirt, my thumb brushing over the line of his braided necklace.

"I'll keep you as long as I can trust you, baby girl. So don't break that trust."

A gut feeling stabs with a sharp pain through my stomach, a knowing ache. It gives me the sense that I'm going to have to prove he can trust me with his life in a much truer way than I'm able to prepare myself for.

Our connection came with far too much ease. I have a sudden feeling that it will be gravely tested... and soon.

CHAPTER NINE
MERRICK

BY SEVEN O'CLOCK this morning, Ethan had a brand-new phone for Willa, my direct number and my emergency line already saved in her contacts. I expect things to go smoothly this morning, meeting up with Gabriel and Benji for negotiations, but you never know when it comes to my business. I like to err on the side of caution, and I wanted to make sure Willa and I had a direct means of communication.

I know my infatuation with her is from the initial chemical burn of finding someone shiny and new. Except she wasn't shiny and new when I found her, and I think it's best that way. She's real—emotional scars and all—and maybe that's how I know that something more than a fleeting chemical burn is on the table for us. She's gotten under my skin, and I feel her crawling.

She's stuck in the back of my mind. The thought of my precious baby girl waiting for me at home simmers in my thoughts, always present and on the threat of boiling over.

I didn't fuck her this morning, though I partially regret

it now. I fucked her enough last night to have her sore and exhausted. She looked too sweet sleeping soundly in my bed to wake her for that. I woke her just long enough to give her the new phone, made sure she could unlock it, and kissed her goodbye.

Now that I'm in the car, on the way to the warehouse for this meeting, I have regrets. I regret that I told her goodbye. I regret that I didn't deepen the kiss when she whimpered for me. I regret that I didn't go down on her, just so I could still have the taste of her on my tongue. I regret not climbing back into bed with her, calling the whole damn meeting off, and making Benji handle it himself.

As if blowing off my boss was ever an option.

It's not as though Benji Baker would ever understand the primal need to be with the woman he claimed. He murdered his last girl, right in front of her best friend, too. He's out on bail right now, but he's being charged with murder, because that best friend is willing to testify—brave little bitch. I don't know anyone who's crossed the Senseless and lived to see their next birthday. I'm certain Benji will be asking me to organize a hit on her before long.

My driver turns onto the dirt path that runs along the metal fencing surrounding the warehouse. I look over at the gray box of a building, my view sliced by the metal loops of the fence as we drive down the path.

The parking lot is empty except for the bright green weeds growing through the cracks, breaking through the fading and chipped yellow lines. The building has been abandoned for years—an old motor factory long since shut down and deserted. We use it as a neutral meeting ground for business dealings that are best handled in person.

I'm fashionably late, ten minutes past the hour we agreed to meet, and though I don't expect to see Benji show up for another five minutes or so, I'm surprised that I don't see another car pulled up to the loading dock—Gabriel should already be here.

I feel a sudden pull to the phone in my pocket, so I take it out. My fingers instantly work to shoot off a text to Willa, feeling some strange sense of urgency to connect with her.

MERRICK: Hope you get some rest, baby girl. I'll see you for lunch.

I don't know what the point of that text was. I already told her I'd be back in time to have lunch with her. She's not just under my skin; she's gotten her claws sunk deep inside me, like I can feel her when I'm not with her, the nagging of her sweet soul calling to me from afar.

My feelings for her are dangerous in my business... but I don't mind a little danger.

My driver, Bryce, pulls up to the loading dock, backing in to ensure we can exit quickly if necessary. I should have brought Ethan with me, but I felt uneasy about leaving

Willa alone, and Ethan's one of the few people I trust fully. He'll take care of her while I'm doing business.

I slip on my sunglasses and step out of the car, walking up the ramp toward the parking lot. I stop, shoving my hands into my pockets and glance around. No one in sight. I look over my shoulder at Bryce and Shawn—another from my security team—and jerk my head toward the side door to the warehouse.

"Let's wait inside." I'd rather not be standing out in the open like this.

We cross the lot to the white side door, and I pull it open. It's unlocked, which it normally is. We don't lock it and no one else is coming out here to do it. The warehouse is empty aside from the old assembly line machinery.

My phone starts ringing just as we step inside, and I pull it from my pocket to answer immediately. Nico's name flashes across the screen, and I know it's urgent if he's calling. He's good with computers and documents, and his hacking skills allow him to provide me intel—not just on my own men, but on the Chaos and their dealings, as well.

I don't even get out my name before Nico rushes to speak. "It's a setup. Get out."

Shit.

"Did you call Benji?"

"Yeah, I already headed him off, but they aren't after him. They want you. I tapped Gabriel's phone calls and he's really pissed that his daughter opened your gift...What did you send him?"

"His dealer's tongue in a box."

"That's fucked-up, man," Nico chuckles just before I hang up—there's no time for social niceties.

My pulse kicks up a notch. "Shit." I turn and rush back to the car. "We've gotta go, it's a setup." Bryce and Shawn run back to the car as I open the back door and slide in. "Hurry." They slip into the front seats, and I buckle my belt.

As the car speeds forward into the parking lot, my thoughts aim at Willa. I know she's in good hands with Ethan, but she'd be in better hands with me—and I fucking left her alone. The thought of something happening to her makes me physically ill. I've obsessively attached myself to her, and my obsessive attachments are permanent. But that means she's at risk, too, because she's mine now.

When I should be pulling out my gun, I'm pulling out my phone instead, pulling up my texts. As if she knows from across the universe, her reply to my earlier text pings through at just this moment.

WILLA: Couldn't go back to sleep after you left. See you at lunch. Be careful.

Be careful.

I didn't know two words could hold the weight of the world, but those two certainly do. She didn't have to reply.

She didn't have to say anything at all. She certainly didn't have to tell me to be careful...but she did, and that's more telling than anything.

Bryce pulls the car back through the opening in the metal fence and turns back down the dirt road that runs alongside the fencing. Punching the gas, he speeds ahead, the car kicking up dust and pebbles as it rumbles over the dirt path.

At the end, he takes a sharp left to turn back onto the main road, and I type out a reply to Willa.

MERRICK: So glad I found you, baby gi

Before I can finish typing the text, another vehicle comes from nowhere and slams into the back end of our SUV, flinging us all forward, then back in our seats. My phone flies out of my hand, lands on the floorboard, and slides beneath the front passenger seat.

"Fuck." I turn my head over my shoulder to look behind us, spotting a large black SUV at our rear, another pulling into the other lane and speeding to drive alongside us.

Shawn pulls out his gun, but it's already too late.

The SUV at our side makes a sharp veer toward us, slamming into the side of our vehicle, and we're pushed toward the small shoulder of the back road that runs alongside a ditch.

UNSEEN

Bryce recovers the vehicle just as the SUV behind slams into the rear again, throwing us forward. As our collective adrenaline peaks, rushing angrily through our veins, we're bumped hard from the side, and this time Bryce loses control.

We skid toward the shoulder and the front tire catches on the edge of the sharp dip that drops into a ditch before the ground meets the tree line. Our SUV is tugged toward that trench at high speed.

It tips.

It rolls.

And the world goes black—but not before I see the flash of Willa's beautiful green eyes in my mind.

CHAPTER TEN
Willa

I'VE BEEN SITTING at the dining room table for half an hour. Merrick should've been here thirty minutes ago for lunch, but he hasn't returned yet. Ethan has locked himself in Merrick's office, and I don't know what's going on, but I can't ignore the nagging feeling that something's wrong.

Merrick is a man of his word—I know that much already—and he told me he would be back for lunch. Lunch is cold now, and Ethan's avoiding me.

I push back my chair and stand, moving quickly to Merrick's office down the hall, where Ethan has locked himself inside. I raise my fist and knock insistently on the door. It takes Ethan nearly thirty seconds to pull it open, and when he does, one look at him tells me that something isn't right.

"Where's Merrick?"

His lips part to speak, he pauses, then sighs. "I guess I can't delay telling you any longer."

"Delay telling me what?"

"Merrick's gone."

Merrick's gone?

"What do you mean?"

"His meeting with the Chaos was an ambush. There was a car wreck. Bryce is dead. Shawn's okay, but has a broken arm. And Merrick is…gone. He was in the car when it rolled and crashed, but he's gone now. We think Gabriel took him alive, but we don't know for sure."

My heart stops, then starts again with a fury. "So…so what are you doing? What are you doing to find him?"

He sighs again, turning away from me and moving to sit behind the desk, looking at a laptop screen. "We've narrowed it down to two possible locations."

"Great, then go to them both. What are you waiting for?"

"It's not that simple."

"I know Merrick's rank. I know his value to the Senseless. You should have everyone out looking for him." My hands are shaking.

"Everyone *is* out looking for him; that's how we've narrowed it down."

Ethan's cell phone rings and he picks it up from the desk. "Yeah?" he says, then pauses. His eyebrows raise as he listens, then he slams his laptop shut and shoves to his feet, sprinting around the desk. "Great, then they must have him at the dealer's house." He breezes past me, heading for the door. "I'll be there in twenty." He ends the call and pockets his phone, charging for the door.

"Ethan!" I call out, and he stops, turning back around to face me. "Tell me. Did they find him?"

"We think so, but we won't know for sure until we get there."

I start walking. "I'm coming with you."

Ethan shakes his head. "No, you aren't. You're staying put."

"Alone? You think Merrick's been kidnapped by a rival cartel and you're going to leave me alone in his home? No. I'm coming."

He pauses, giving me a once over as he thinks it through. "He'll kill me if I take you. It's dangerous."

I charge past him. "He'll understand. The alternative isn't any safer. I'd be an easy target here." I walk until I reach the front door and then I stop, turning to wait for him.

He sighs in resignation as he walks past me and opens the front door—I think he must do a lot of sighing working for a man like Merrick, and he's about to do a lot more with a woman like me around. "I can't win here," he says. "He's gonna be pissed at me either way."

"I'll tell him to go easy on you," I say, stepping out onto the porch.

I flinch against the sunlight. It's excessively bright today. Ethan reaches into his jacket pocket and retrieves a pair of sunglasses, handing them over to me. I slip them on quickly.

"I really don't know who the fuck you are or where you came from, Willa. But I suppose we can figure out how to get along if you're willing to go to bat for Merrick."

"He saved me," I tell Ethan. "I can save him, too."

ADRENALINE FLOODS MY veins and my heart hammers heavily against my ribs. I look up at the sleek house at the edge of Lake Erie—the one with the familiar sharp lines and glass walls that look out at the softly rippling water. It's not just anyone's house, it's the house where I was kept captive, locked in the dark basement for so, so long... it's Ryan's house.

This is where Ethan and his team think Merrick is being held, and they have to go in and check it out. But fear pulses through every beat of my heart as I gaze up at the house from a quarter mile away.

Our car and two others—filled with men from the Senseless—are parked in the grass beneath the shade of trees, down the hill which leads up to Ryan's house, just off the dirt path.

It *was* Ryan's house.

I have to remind myself that he's dead. I saw his corpse with my own eyes.

"Stay in the car," Ethan tells me, loading his gun.

I drag my eyes from the house and turn my head to look over at him in the driver's seat beside me. "No. I'm coming in." I unbuckle my seatbelt and reach for the door.

Ethan's hand snaps out to grip my wrist. "*No.* Stay in the car. You won't be any help inside; you'll just get in the way."

"I won't get in the way. If Merrick's hurt, he'll need me—"

"If he's hurt, he'll need medical attention, and we need to get him out fast. Somehow, I don't think a reunion with the girl he's fucking is going to get him out any quicker."

"I'm not just a girl he's fucking."

"What *are* you, then?"

"I-I don't know yet. But I'm more than that."

The team in the car ahead of us gets out, slamming doors shut, loading guns, and preparing to go in.

Ethan sighs, letting go of my wrist. "Assuming he's still alive, I know he'll be glad to see you here waiting for him. Be here so you can be with him when we get him out. If you go in there, you're more likely to get yourself killed than anything else. Stay here and stay safe, and you can be what he needs through recovery. Okay?"

Ethan looks at me expectantly, and resigned, I give him a slow nod. What he's saying is logical—it makes sense. Yet the rising anger within me feeds irrationality, my heart still thumping with the impulse to run up that hill and save Merrick myself.

Ethan reaches into his pocket and pulls something out. He flicks his wrist and a knife pops open—a switchblade.

"Hang onto this," he tells me. "If anyone you don't recognize shows up, stab first and ask questions later. Got it?"

I nod.

Ethan gets out of the car and I watch as five or six men gather. They talk for a minute, and then they're gone, walking across the grass beneath the trees.

What if Merrick's already dead?

The thought is heavy, far heavier than it should be, given that I've only known this man for a matter of days. Yet the thought of him being gone twists the sharp stabbing pain in my chest. I rub my palm over my heart as a painful image fills my mind. It's an image of Merrick trapped, chained, hurt, and broken, like I'd been for far too long.

It brings unexpected tears to my eyes to think of something bad happening to him. The sadness of it swells in my chest, forcing out all the air from my lungs and leaving no room for the next breath.

A small cry escapes me, and it's stupid, I know it is. I shouldn't feel anything. Maybe if I were smarter, I would use this as an opportunity to get away and go back to the minimum wage, lonely, depressed life I had before.

Except I haven't felt lonely or depressed since Merrick found me.

I want to stay with him.

I want to *be* with him.

But a girl can't just choose to be with a man like Merrick Shaw... she has to prove her worth.

I promised him I would prove he could trust me with his life, and this is the perfect opportunity. His life is on the line, and here I am, knife in hand, at the location where he's likely being held hostage.

Go.

The word bursts in my mind and my body obeys. I open the car door, jump out, slam it shut behind me, and take off running. I sprint, running full speed until I catch up with Ethan and two other Senseless men as they creep in toward the side of the garage.

"What the fuck are you doing?" Ethan whispers. "I told you to stay put!"

I'm not about to argue with him. I simply turn my gaze to the small window just above our heads at the side of the garage. "Give me a boost and I can sneak in through that window."

"I'm not letting you—"

"Is there time to argue about this, Ethan? Just give me a boost. I'll go in and open the back door so the rest of you can come in."

He stares at me blankly, blinking, with a curious and confused expression on his face. A few moments pass, and then he shakes his head before stepping forward. "Fuck, fine. But you'd better tell him you forced me to do this."

"I'll tell him whatever you want if you'll just get me inside that house."

Ethan and one of the men hold their hands together for

me to step on, boosting me up as I reach for the window's ledge. They're able to get me high enough that my face is aligned with the glass, and I peek inside first, noting there are two cars parked in the garage, the light is off, and there doesn't appear to be any movement.

I draw my fingers along the edge of the window, searching for a spot I can hook my finger and pull it open with. Eventually, I'm able to tug, and I'm relieved to find that the window is unlocked. It pops open, swinging out toward me. It doesn't open all the way to a right angle, but it opens wide enough that I think I can shimmy through.

"Higher," I tell them beneath me, and they push me up.

I have to ignore the roar of adrenaline whooshing through my veins, pulsing behind my ears as I push my arm and head through the small opening. I hook my armpit over the ledge as I climb one foot up the siding. The men beneath give a heavy push at the bottom of my other foot to hoist me higher, giving me enough momentum to slip through to my torso, teetering on the ledge.

Thankfully, there's a table beneath the window on the inside of the garage. It's high enough that I can touch it with the tips of my fingers as I rock my body forward. I take a quick breath before pitching my weight headfirst, letting my body fall toward the bench. My palms land flat, and I manage to guide myself down, wiggling one leg through, then the other, before dropping my feet to land heavily on the table.

I freeze, tensing every muscle to stillness, waiting to make sure no one inside the house heard me or will be coming after me. When I'm sure we're in the clear, I climb down from the table, touching the ground softly with my feet. I circle the cars and move to the door that leads inside the house. I step up onto the landing in front of the door and wrap my hand around the knob.

I jerk my hand back with a snap as a phantom shock shoots from the knob through my palm.

I remember coming through this door once before. I remember fighting Ryan and his girlfriend as they pulled me out of the trunk of his car in this very garage. I remember screaming, thrashing, fighting for my life as they dragged me through the door—*this* door.

I blow out a breath, shake my head, and bring the image of Merrick chained and tortured to my mind.

It hardens me again, steels me.

I grab the knob and turn, and thankfully, the door opens. I peek my head inside slowly, glancing around to see if anyone is there.

I don't hear any voices.

I don't see any movement.

Still, I know I need to be cautious.

Slowly, I open the door and step lightly into the mudroom. I close the door quietly behind me, thinking I should leave everything as I found it, just in case. I creep ahead, cautiously turning the corner and finding myself in the kitchen.

It's clean. No dishes are out, no pots or pans on the stove. All the lights are off, and I find comfort in that darkness.

It seems like no one is here. It seems like someone came through and cleaned the place after Merrick killed Ryan, and they left it spotless. But Merrick is supposed to be here.

So if he's here, then where is he?

Nausea rolls through my stomach as two words float into my mind... *The basement.*

Ryan had it all set up for a hostage with locks and chains and sound-proofing. I get it now. It makes sense why they would bring Merrick here. They could lock him alone in that basement and no one would ever find him there.

Except his men knew—the Senseless are smarter than the Chaos. I feel some odd sense of pride in that, as if I've already accepted that I'm becoming one of them.

I belong with them. I belong with the Senseless because I belong with Merrick Shaw.

I startle, jumping and whirling around at the sound of gunfire coming from outside the house, followed by shouting, and even more gunfire.

What do I do?

Do I open the door to let Ethan and the others inside? Or will that just open the door for the Chaos?

I pause, close my eyes, and when I open them again, I know what I need to do.

I need to get Merrick.

I turn and run down the hallway, quickly finding the door to the basement.

Just as my fingers graze the knob, someone shouts, "Hey!"

My head snaps to the side to see a man at the far end of the hall. He's not Senseless, I know it, though he looks oddly familiar. I let go of the doorknob and step back, raising my hands in surrender, though I'm not ready to surrender.

"Drop it," the man says, and I look at my hand, remembering I'm still holding Ethan's switchblade.

I try to let go of it, but I can't bring myself to. If I drop it, I'll be defenseless... defenseless and at the mercy of a strange man in the same house where I was tortured.

"Just put it down, and I won't hurt you," he says, gun aimed directly at me.

"Just bend over and let me do it. I won't hurt you."

I remember his voice as the words flash through my mind. He's one of Ryan's sick friends who would use me at his parties.

I feel the way my expression hardens, pain and anger rising and showing themselves in my features. My grip on the knife tightens.

I watch as he recalls, as his own memories creep back into his dark mind. He tilts his head to the side as he slowly walks toward me, a grin lifting the corner of his mouth.

"Oh, hey, I remember you... the bitch in the basement.

Wondered what happened to you after Ryan died."

My eyes dart to the basement door and back again.

"You miss it?" he says, chuckling darkly. "Baby, if you want someone to chain you up in the basement again, I'll be happy to help with that." He lowers his gun, as if he doesn't perceive me to be a threat... as if he really thinks I'm just trying to go back to the basement to be chained up.

How is he so stupid?

His men are fighting off Senseless outside, and he doesn't immediately realize that I'm with them?

He walks toward me and I let him, I let him come as close as he dares.

"Give me that knife, baby. I don't want you to hurt yourself."

Rage boils inside me, but I pretend I'm calm, pretend that I'm complacent and obedient, pretend that I'm the girl Ryan broke me to be.

But I'm not that girl today.

And I won't be that girl ever again.

I wait until he's close before slowly lowering my arms, pretending I've given up. And when he's close enough that I can reach out and touch him, I don't hesitate, I don't think. I pull my arm back, knife in hand, and shove it into his stomach, hard and fast and deep. His body curls around the knife, his eyes going wide as he looks at me with astonishment.

I jerk my arm back hard to pull the knife out, then

thrust it forward again, again, again. My chest is heaving; I'm panting, breathing in violent energy that fuels me in taking back control of my life.

Ryan and his friends don't win.

I win.

I step back, watching as the man who's name I don't remember slumps to the floor, slipping to his knees before falling sideways. Panting, I lean over him as his eyes slowly close.

"I'm *not* your baby," I practically spit the words down at him. "There's only one man who gets to call me that. I belong to Merrick Shaw."

I belong to Merrick Shaw.

Saying the words out loud is cathartic, releasing a strange calm that makes me feel more in control, more powerful. I belong to that man, and belonging to him makes me stronger.

The gunfire I'd been ignoring still erupts outside the house, and I know I need to move quickly. I don't let go of the knife, though it's getting harder to hold on to with my hand coated in slick blood.

I reach for the knob and pull open the basement door. Darkness greets me, flowing up from the basement as if it could be carried on a breeze. It's frightening, but familiar—familiar enough that I run to it.

I sprint down the steps and quickly find the light switch, flipping on the light from the single bulb that hangs eerily from the ceiling. The light comes on and the sight before me is like a lightning bolt to the heart.

Merrick is chained in the same place where he found me. His arms are strung above him and stretched out in a V, and his feet just graze the floor. He's shirtless, bruised, and bleeding. His chest and stomach are covered with small cuts from his collarbone to his pelvis, blood dripping from each wound.

The crimson is dark and dried in places, but a few cuts still ooze fresh blood that runs all the way down his front, pooling at his belt buckle, some of it soaking into his pants. His head is dropped forward and there's a small black hood covering his head.

I rush for him, grab the hood, and tear it off. He flinches and blinks, jerking his arms as if he's preparing to fight me.

"Merrick," I whisper his name. "Merrick, it's me."

He goes still, rigid, blinking and taking in the sight of me. "Willa?"

"Hi," I say stupidly, the look of his light brown eyes warming and calming me instantly.

"Why are you here? Did they take you?"

"No, no. I came with Ethan and your men, but they're..." I glance over my shoulder toward the stairs. "I think they're in trouble outside. I snuck in before the gunfire started."

"Gunfire?" He jerks his arms. "Get me down. I need to get you out of here." That's when his eyes fall to my hand, still holding the knife with blood dripping from my soaked arm. "Are you hurt?"

"I think I cut my hand, but I'm okay. I think I killed him." I look up at the chains, following the path of them along the track in the ceiling, walking along to find the end. They're locked to a ring that's nailed securely into the cement wall, and I whirl around, trying to figure out what I'm going to do.

"Baby, go hide in the corner. I need you out of sight."

"I'm not leaving you here alone. And I'm not going to hide."

"Willa, don't argue—"

"Merrick!" I hear Ethan's voice from somewhere upstairs, and the flood of relief is instant. "Willa!"

I run halfway up the steps to call to him, and Merrick shouts at me, but I ignore him. "Here!" I shout up to Ethan, then run back down to wait.

I move in front of Merrick, in the spotlight glow of the single lightbulb. My fist tightens around the handle of the knife, ready to fight if someone else comes down those steps instead of Ethan.

I'll kill anyone who tries to hurt Merrick.

Thankfully, it's Ethan who appears at the top of the steps. He and a couple of his men come rushing down to meet us.

"We've got ten minutes tops to get the fuck out of here. Get him out of those chains," Ethan says, and his men start working to get Merrick down. "Did you kill that guy at the top of the stairs?" Ethan scans me with wide eyes.

I nod. "Yeah. I didn't really have a choice."

"Good. Well, I'm glad you're not dead. Two of ours outside are down, but we got three of theirs. Gabriel got away."

"I don't really care," I say, spinning to face Merrick. "I just want to bring Merrick home."

Merrick doesn't say a word as he gazes at me, holding my stare. The gray flecks in his light brown eyes shimmer and shift in the spotlight, and I think they must reflect something shifting within him, too.

The shift is permanent, a reflection of confirmed commitment and loyalty. It's a confirmation that he sees me for who I really am and what I could become for him. I want to become those things for him.

I want to become *everything* for him.

The chains loosen before giving way, letting his arms drop to his sides. He wobbles a bit with the shift of his weight as he drops fully onto his feet. I let my knife drop from my hand, hearing it clatter against the cement floor as I lunge forward to catch him.

He doesn't really need me to catch him. He steadies quickly, and then his palms find my cheeks, lifting my face to look at me clearly, blood smearing over both of us.

"I see you, baby girl, the real you, and you're mine," he says it too quietly for anyone else to hear. He presses his forehead to mine and I sigh in relief at the touch of him.

UNSEEN

"Our dark shades match so perfectly."

I smile, letting my eyes flutter shut. "That's where you found me… in the dark."

"I did. And you found me the same way."

EPILOGUE
MERRICK

six months later

WILLA OFTEN COMES to my office when I'm working, and when she does, I can't finish a fucking phone call without ordering her to her knees with my eyes. She comes to me because she wants it, and I fail to tell her no every damn time. I've become quite skilled with edging my release on the longer calls, waiting until it's ended so I can pull her up, fuck her, and finish inside her.

I've just hung up with Benji—he was shot about five months ago the night before his murder trial, and the world speculates whether he's dead. He's very much alive, but he's in hiding.

We let the media make their assumptions that I'm now the highest-ranking member of the Senseless, let the feds think we're weakened when we're stronger than ever. And Willa, though she's faceless and nameless in the media, is the queen at my side.

I wrap my hand around my queen's neck and urge her

to her feet, then reach down to lift her skirt over her hips. I'm not surprised to find she's bare beneath—no panties—because I know she came in here with one goal. I shove her back to push her ass up onto the edge of my desk as she pants, the skin around her lips flushed pink from sucking my cock.

"Wear the mask?" she asks me with heat in her gaze.

That's new.

With a smirk, I reach across my desk and grab the white plastic face mask the Senseless often wear. "This?"

She licks her lips and nods. "Yeah."

"You want me to wear this while I fuck you, baby girl?"

She nods some more, leaning back on her palms and spreading her knees for me.

I stretch the elastic band and lift the mask over my head, settling it in place to cover my face with only my eyes visible behind the two holes. Stepping in between her legs, I slip my hand over her hip, reaching around to dig my fingers into her flesh, which has thickened up quite nicely since I took her from the piece of shit who starved her. I fist my cock, lining it up and rubbing the tip along her wet slit.

She moans, letting her head fall back, and her hand reaches aimlessly along the desktop. At least, I think it's aimless until her palm lands on the switchblade I make her carry around for her own protection.

"Use this on me," she pants, lifting her hand and holding it out for me.

A dark chuckle escapes me as I take it from her hand. Willa's devolution from broken girl, to curious submissive, to dark and reckless little masochist is perhaps the most beautiful fucking thing I've ever witnessed. She chose to become one of us, embracing that she's one of the Senseless whole-heartedly—and that means embracing our shameless depravity.

I knew what she had the potential to become from the moment I laid eyes on her. I've enjoyed watching the darkness take hold of her over the last six months. She was once lost in it, broken by it. But she embraced it when she killed a man to save my life and let herself become who she was always meant to be.

Mine.

And I'm fucking in love with her.

I flip open the blade and she whimpers, her thick tits sharply rising and falling with her panted breaths. I grab hold of her dress at the center of her chest and tug it away from her skin, then use the knife to puncture a hole. I tear it apart, ripping from both sides of the hole with my hands to expose her. Her dark nipples are already hard nubs that beg to be teased.

I turn the blade and carefully drag the flat side of the metal over the peak of her nipple. Her body is rigid and tense, and a shiver ripples through her as I pull the blade away.

"Hold still, baby girl." I carefully press the tip into her

skin between her breasts, just a scratch, dragging it down to make a quick, sharp nick.

She cries out at the burn, and her bright red blood pools, ready to spill between her breasts. I can't take it. I slam the knife down on the desk, grip her hips with both hands, and slam my cock inside her, eyes fixed on the blood running down her center.

I keep the mask on while I fuck her hard, making us both come by the time the blood has slipped all the way down to the dark curls over her sex.

I knew from the moment I met her that she'd be the woman for me.

I would bleed for her.

And now I know she'll bleed for *me*.

THANK YOU FOR READING WILLA & MERRICK'S STORY!
MORE FROM THE SENSELESS WORLD IS COMING.

Be sure to follow me on social media
so you don't miss any updates.

IF YOU'RE READY FOR SOMETHING A LITTLE DARKER,
CHECK OUT MY DYSTOPIAN DARK ROMANCE TRILOGY...

ember glen

USA TODAY BESTSELLING AUTHOR
BRYNN FORD

The trilogy is complete and ready for you to binge read!
Start with book one...

spark of madness

CONNECT WITH BRYNN

Author Newsletter
brynnford.com/connect

Goodreads
goodreads.com/brynnfordauthor

BookBub
bookbub.com/profile/brynn-ford

Instagram
@brynnfordauthor
instagram.com/brynnfordauthor

TikTok
@brynnfordauthor
tiktok.com/@brynnfordauthor

Facebook Page
facebook.com/brynnfordauthor

Brynn's Daring Darlings
(Facebook Group)
bit.ly/brynnsdarlings

BRYNN'S BOOKS

THE FOUR FAMILIES TRILOGY
Counts of Eight
Dance with Death
Pas de Trois

THE FOUR FAMILIES SPIN-OFF
King of Masters

EMBER GLEN
Spark of Madness
Blaze of Misery
Embers of Mercy

SENSELESS
(Novellas)
Unheard
Unseen

STANDALONES
Jagged Line Paradise
Sugar Wood

ABOUT THE AUTHOR

Brynn Ford is a USA Today Bestselling Author of dark romance for daring readers. She writes emotionally heavy love stories that will twist your soul and shatter your heart before pulling you back together with a hopeful happily-ever-after.

Brynn's books are dark, sometimes disturbing, and often overwhelming. But they're always brightened by an insistent, spicy romance that will live rent-free in your head long after you've turned the final page.

When Brynn isn't obsessively writing, you may find her binge-watching favorite shows while eating far too much junk food or fanatically reading, always seeking to lose herself in the emotional roller coaster of a damn good story. She's a firm believer that her characters continue to live outside the pages in the minds of her readers. Stories don't end just because there aren't any more pages to turn.

Made in the USA
Columbia, SC
07 June 2024

36826520R00086